Drop

H.D. KIRKLAND, III

"Between the conception and the creation, between the emotion and the response, falls the shadow." ~T.S. Elliot

ISBN - 9781733554039

DEDICATION

For my family and friends, they all consist of the best. My wife, Amy, is the energy within my heart. My parents struggled with me all my life but their love overwhelmed my rebellion. Thank you all putting up with me.

ACKNOWLEDGMENTS

Headland High School and all of their teachers.

Troy University of Dothan and their incredible staff .

All of you smokers that let me bum a cigarette all those times I was broke. You guys are awesome.

CHAPTER 1

The Beginning

To lose one's mind is insufferable, yet, sometimes it suffices for one to just not mind.

Prophets only see parts of a great picture, like particles of dreams left to scurry across the channels of the mind. It is an arduous experience and an enduring task to try and discern accurate ideas of what they've seen. These infinitesimal traces of the subconscious are held together by an intricate web of metaphors and sometimes nightmarish visages. The grip that fastens the mind in the wake can haunt it forever, while the meaning gets lost in madness.

I am no prophet, and never claimed to be, but I understand what I was shown. The only night worth remembering in my life is the only night I try to forget. It was a night I lived with even before I lived it. It was the night I met the shadow within myself - the part of me that had been whispering violent noises that foreshadowed that night with subtle and inconspicuous caresses.

There are some that believe that within the collective conscious of our species lies the ability to evolve into greater beings – a more enlightened and special kind of breed connected consciously to each cell within themselves. The theory rests on the mind and its ability to evolve subconsciously. Perceivably, this harmonic transcendence shatters the shadow within the mind, setting us free from our bondage within. It is seen to be a rebirth – a shedding of the old skin suffocating our souls, but what lies beneath the shadow is something not so easily shattered, nor meant to be found. It is far better to lose your mind than to find it there, for then it is no longer yours.

The shadow is wholly within us all, but also wholly apart from us. It is the shroud hiding the most primordial level of our subconscious; concealing that which lies dormant like a patient predator ready to devour the mind. Though the shadow is there, it is not impervious. It can be broken, hence the terrible transcendence, and what awaits is not born unto us by our subconscious but rather not a part of us at all, just within us – hidden and shackled within the dark cave our conscious. In a sense, if the transcendence becomes us, it can be construed as some strange stage of evolution; or as a divine inheritance of that which is evil.

I am a witness to what slithers in the muddy depths beneath the conscious.

I sat face to face to that which is hidden in me.

And it spoke to me.

CHAPTER 2

The Start of a Journey for No Good Reason

It was Saturday on the first day of fall in the year 2000. The weather was hardly identifiable as cool while fleeting traces of summer still echoed in the wind. It was the ideal time of year to ride with your windows down, the air shut-off, and the music loud enough to leave a permanent bruise on your soul. Everywhere, trees were still cloaked by leaves that had not yet been divested by the raging cold of winter which was steadily upon us. Flowers still held on to their attractive colors and had not yet slipped into the withering stage of their cycle. Everything appeared perfect, in fact.

I lived in a town called Threscia. It was named after the wife of a pioneer named John Tott, who was said to have fought in the Revolutionary War while just a young boy. It was a farming town bordering the booming city of Crepes in the southeast corner of Alabama. It was home to simple people living not so simple lives. It is a town where you will rarely ever hear a complaint unless it involves football or politics. In 2000, it was a place where Bush/Cheney signs were as abundant as the Confederate flags decorating yards and houses.

Almost all the roads that scar the body of Threscia either lead to or away from town. The further that you venture into the bowels of the country, away from the vermillion brick homes and the manicured lawns in town, your mind could easily be dizzied by the vast green fields that opened wide in acres of land, grazed by the lazy cattle always looking down, it seemed. A tall sea of crowded forests looms over the miles of narrow veins of asphalt winding through the countryside.

In Threscia not much ever happens. Occasionally, news of a snake bite excites conversation for a while or some old lady may fall and arouse concern, but rarely anything happens to pull the residents of town into the arms of fear and distress. The exception occurred in 1994 when a posse of delinquents, bored and twisted on air-duster fumes, vandalized the Baptist church by painting a descriptive caricature of Satan swallowing a human man. The disturbing image depicted his legs limply dangling from the vicious mouth and a crazed look from Satan's eyes. This inevitably caused a contagious strain of mass paranoia.

Suddenly, fear of devil worship and baby sacrifice spread through the town like herpes at a frat party. It all ended when a confiscated note passed between several students detailed the events perfectly incriminating four thirteen-year-old boys. They were berated viciously by most everyone in town and were consequently expelled from school and sent to the Adolescent Center for Delinquents. As astounding as it would've been to have had a coven of hard-core Satanists running amuck and begetting some holy war pitting demon-loving brother against angel-loving sister in a fight to the death, realistically Threscia is a mundane town.

At that point, the town was removed from anything appealing to the masses of our culture, such as the enticing acts of ritualized torture and/or murder/suicide. That would change much later.

.....

I was slowly approaching the town, stoned and barely awake at around five in the afternoon. For some of us just turning twenty and avid fiends for the night, this was the dawn of every new day and normal. My best friend, Hess, was with me and muttered something inaudible over my music forcing me to turn down Pantera's 'Shedding Skin' which had been thundering in my head like a breaking tsunami wave to keep me somewhat conscious at the time.

"What, dammit?" I asked in confusion as I continued staring straight ahead at the road while gradually creeping to a forlorn stop sign peppered by bird-shot.

"Maybe you should put that away before we get there," he said pointing at my hand resting in my lap.

I had admittedly zoned out for what may have been several long minutes while admiring the delicate thrashing of the music. I looked down and discovered that I had been babysitting a plump joint we had been sharing.

"Jesus!" I exclaimed angrily, "You're right, man. That could've been disastrous. A damnable catastrophic dilemma even!"

I fumbled at the ashtray with my fingertips, forcing it open. Then I dropped the roach inside, slamming it shut quickly. It is a fact, a rule even, that these things just happen and you learn to move on. Hess understood this, which is why he only laughed slightly as he puffed a cigarette and turned the music back up.

A minute later we breached the center of town. There are roughly a dozen conservatively structured buildings for commerce that make a square around a plain enough park. The park was shaded with Oak and Magnolia trees, garnished with a variety of flowers, and cradled an impressive fountain of frozen children playing giddily in the water as it sprayed. The scene was punctuated by a rustic gazebo crafted nearly one hundred fifty years ago. Since everything was within walking distance, visitors either strolled leisurely or cruised at low speed on a one-way street feeding around the park and back onto the main street.

I parked in front of the building which served as a home for both the sheriff's department and town hall. It was a new building and its white bricks still appeared as immaculate and pristine as the day that they had been laid. Located between Kathy's Kitchen and Red House Books on the north end of the square directly behind the large fountain in the park, it was a significant upgrade the sheriff's office of my youth. A few years ago, the citizens of Theresia agreed progressive, yet slow, growth was necessary, so a single more modernized building was erected replacing the portable building just outside the square.

I knew walking into the Sheriff's Department completely stoned was not the brightest example of things to do. I had, though, become quite skilled at the delicate art of disguising exactly how high I actually was, or that I was even high at all, for that matter. Even though my mind was numb, speaking clearly was never a problem for me. Having the right focus, honestly, is the most important aspect. Also, I found that keeping an intense devotion to eye contact always reinforces the legitimacy of being responsible; certainly not a filthy doper. By trial and error, I perfected this rare art form of deceitful sobriety.

Hess, on the other hand, may as well have had a joint pinched tight between his lips and a bong shoved high up in his ass because he couldn't have disguised the fact he was stoned from Helen Keller. So, naturally, I berated him as casually as I knew how and forced him to stay in the car.

I entered the main lobby through a pair of spotless glass doors. Immediately, the pleasurable aroma of fresh linen assaulted my senses. At a glance, I noticed the Glade Plug-Ins exerting the precious smell from the outlets in each wall. The tile floor appeared slick and glistened; gleaming like the belly of a wet baby seal. The fluorescent lights burning above bounced a sharp reflection off of the tile. It bent and stretched like some rubbery laser before exploding through the lobby and was thrown into the bibulous tanned walls, making them shine like the tile floor. It was a nightmare for anyone who was stoned.

There were two separate windows. On the left, in the back corner of the wall, was a compartmentalized office space behind a glass window where one could ask questions or pay their utility bill to the short, obese woman caged inside. There was no one at the desk today because the office was closed on Saturdays. However, straight ahead was a larger area protected by plexiglass that stretched from one wall to the other. Behind it was the dispatch station and to the right was a heavy, securely locked door guarding a long hall leading to the Sheriff's office, a break room, and a small holding cell.

Behind the plexiglass surrounded by an assortment of knobs and switches was a beautiful, long-haired Native-American woman named Claire. She had been the dispatcher for Sheriff Kahn since 1997 and was well known in town especially for her gorgeous features. Her straight black hair reached past her shoulder blades. It was so perfectly black that it could only be compared to an abyss void of any distracting blemish. Her dark complexion and deep brown eyes always seemed to lull me into a helpless state of utter confusion.

Ahead of me was an old lady clutching an expensive purse in the crease of her wrinkled elbow. She stood hunched over speaking through a sliding window panel with a hole in it. I recognized her as Mrs. Brown, the wife of the longtime Baptist preacher. There was some sort of dilemma involving her cat and she needed it resolved as soon as possible. I took a seat to wait my turn in one of the uncomfortable hard chairs against the wall. As she droned on with no end in sight, I could see in Claire's face that annoyance was taking hold.

"All I know is that Mr. Tinkle never leaves the yard. He never has," she declared. "He's much too old and besides he's been neutered."

She exasperated a deep and depressed sigh to accentuate her worry. I'm not sure if she ever really expected anything to be done about her missing cat or if it was just that the idea of someone else being aware of and sharing her concern consoled her apprehension.

Her gaze shifted to the many knobs and array of buttons on the console behind Claire. She pointed to the old-school microphone propped on a tiny stand and asked in a demanding tone, "Well can't you get on your thingy back there and call it in? His name is Mr. Tinkle. He's black and white. Twelve years ...."

I was somewhat amused and even infatuated with the old woman's audacious consistency to push her insistence. Claire, however, was not and was on the verge of either blowing her lid and spewing all kinds of colorful insults or laughing hysterically at her nonsensical reluctance to realize the non-existent brevity of her minute dilemma in comparison to other matters that were possibly at hand.

But before Claire could do any of those things, Mrs. Brown's purse began to ring in an obnoxious tone which sounded like dozens of sirens blending together in unison. She dug around in it absent-mindedly until she eventually found a Nokia flip phone. But instead of answering it and ending its assault on the ears of anyone within earshot, she held it before her and squinted her eyes at the keys to see who was calling. Mrs. Brown finally found the 'accept call' button. A moment later she made a comedy show of finding "end call" button.

"I'm afraid I have to go; my sister is stuck on the toilet. Please pass on my concerns to the Sheriff. I assure you that I will be back in touch."

"Yes, ma'am. I hope that your sister is okay," Claire said forcing a smile.

With that, Mrs. Brown turned to leave. As she passed, she glowered at me with an air reminiscent of the Wicked Witch of the West as she scoffed faintly under her dry breath. Perhaps, I thought, it was my fantastical White Zombie t-shirt displaying toothless redneck-like monsters with fleshy eyeballs bulging graphically from their misshaped skulls that she found to be distasteful. "There's usually at least one that tests you," Claire declared through the tiny slot. "That makes four today so far."

"Really?" I said pretending to be amused, but rather just nervous. "Yeah, apparently everyone's cat in town decided to run away."

Frustration was seeping through her pores and staining her expression; changing the tone of her voice.

As she talked all I could do was think of how superbly astonishing she looked. I felt I had to say something so as to not appear a jackass. "That's strange," I managed.

"That's one way of putting it," she joshed. After a very palpable and excruciatingly unpleasant time of silence she finally spoke again, "I think Jacob is back there. Want me to let him know you're here?"

I was an idiot. A wretched stoner – confused and awkward. "Yeah, sure. If you don't mind."

I thanked her as she dismissed herself and disappeared through a side door. Moments later, the locks on the heavy door guarding the control room clicked and clanked as they disengaged causing the door to swing open. Jacob and his father appeared from the other side – Jacob in front followed by Sheriff Kahn. Jacob was smiling nervously as he often did, his eyes broadened by the thick lenses of a pair of black glasses. His sandy blonde hair was parted neatly down the middle and was just long enough to tuck behind his ears. He was pale and skinny, not very tall at all, and wore a Pearl Jam t-shirt with jeans meticulously torn at the knees.

Following closely behind, Sheriff Kahn lurked like a monster. The badge he wore on his pressed uniform winked as the light skied across its smooth surface. His leather holster groaned with each step he took. The marine-style hair-cut and bulky cop-physique would make any criminal think twice about trying him.

As always, he eyed me suspiciously.

After a brief, appropriated, greeting Sheriff Kahn said bluntly, "Jacob tells me that you boys are going to a jazz festival in Pensacola and that you're coming back tomorrow." He presented the statement as more of an interrogation.

I was unaware that Jacob had fed his father this lie and was quite surprised that he had.

"Jazz," I thought? "What the hell?" I tried not to hesitate while silently cursing Jacob silently for putting me in this predicament with no time for preparation. I cleared my throat and said, "Yes sir. If we can find a place to stay; if not, we'll just come straight back."

His eyes shifted slightly, perhaps an indication that he wasn't purely convinced. Jacob must have noticed this too because his eyes fleeted away from his father's glance.

"Who's playing there?" He continued interrogating casually.

"Well," I said convincingly enough, "it's Free Jazz and all those dudes are pretty much anonymous."

I tried to sell this with a half-hearted laugh that teetered closely on the level of two friends just shooting the shit together. From the corner of my eye, I could see Jacob fidgeting suspiciously.

Even from behind her cage of glass, I could sense Claire eyeing me with suspicion.

Sheriff Kahn looked at me in the same stale way a madman might blankly stare at himself in the mirror unsure of anything that's going on. After a moment of internal deliberation, he turned to Jacob and put his hand on his shoulder saying, "Okay. I'm trusting you. If anything happens you call me. Have fun and be careful."

Jacob shrugged sheepishly, "Okay. I know dad. I will."

I could tell that he was a little embarrassed of his dad showing concern and emotion in front of me. It was evident in the way that they interacted that they were closer than most father and sons our age. They were certainly closer than my father and I ever had been. Perhaps this was because for the previous eleven years it had been just the two of them together. When Jacob was only six, his mother had been diagnosed with aggressive stomach cancer. It was a terrible and unfair battle for all three to have suffered.

The sheriff turned to me and pointed jokingly saying, "And you. You be nice."

I laughed legitimately enough and said, "I'll try. Those jazz guys can be dickheads though."

There was a brief stint of chuckling. Sheriff Kahn turned his attention back to Jacob. "Okay then. You boys get goin'." He opened his arms for a hug and Jacob obliged. "I love you."

"I love you too, dad."

.....

When we left the Sheriff's station, the sun was beginning to set. An auburn haze had nestled in the sky and the thick clouds were like dark chunks of some monolithic shadow frozen in place. Hess had been waiting in the car patiently, smoking a cigarette. He let Jacob in the back seat and before we had gotten very far, he began talking.

He couldn't help being a borderline obnoxious fiend; it was just his character.

I'm not sure if anyone could ever really understand Hess or his contradictory personality. Even when I was sure I knew him he somehow obliterated my understanding. He was both athletic and smart, but he was more than reluctant to give a shit about anything. He was irascible and boisterous to the point of exceeding normalcy, yet he was easy to get along with – just so long as he liked you. His attitude was completely shitty which made him hilarious to be around in public settings as he made complete strangers uncomfortable.

The first time I met him was the first day of school in sixth grade. He was new to our school and picked a fight with me. I bloodied his nose and he split my lower lip. We tussled on the gymnasium floor like two amateur wrestlers until the teacher broke us up.

We have been inseparable since.

If nothing else, I could always count on him to get me into some kind of trouble - usually, it was fighting. It was his mouth, which orchestrated, more than anything, his abrasive and shitty, I-don't-give-a-fuck attitude, that landed us in many perilous circumstances. I had my ass kicked by a group of madmen while I was alone just because it was well known that he was my best friend.

There are innumerable unexplainable things in the world, but perhaps the most phenomenal mystery is how two clashing personalities somehow interact in harmony? Whatever the answer is, Hess and I are living examples to its validity.

It was on a curvy road leading us to the outskirts of town, where men can behave as beasts and have fun getting away with it, that during Hess' neurotic chanting I heard him say "Chris" and then the word "acid" both in the same sentence.

"What?" I asked. "What the hell did you just say, man? Chris has acid?"

"Well yeah man," Hess said rubbing his hand on the short fibers of his shaved head, "I told you yesterday that he was getting it. Remember? Jacob is going to trip too, finally." He turned around in the seat and jokingly said to Jacob, "if you don't pussy out this time."

I did not remember this at all. How could I have neglected to learn something of such importance? I must have been involved in the seriousness of the crazed and delusional inner-spinning of my mind. Often, I would go on and on, back and forth with some imaginative dialogue partner during a stoned stupor. When this happened, it was completely possible that the sun could swallow the earth in a blistering gulp and I wouldn't have known.

"No way you told me this, man! I would remember something like that," I declared to convince myself.

Hess scoffed, "Yeah I did, you fucker! You were probably zoned out thinking about frogs humping giant lady-bugs or some goofy shit like that."

He and Jacob both laughed.

"He did tell you. I heard him." Jacob said.

It all began to make sense now. I understood why Jacob had lied to his dad; he didn't want any chance of him checking up on us. Drinking beer and smoking weed at a campfire is one thing, but tripping is a completely different beast altogether. When you're fighting off savage and intense psychedelic enhancements from your mind, your sheriff father is the absolute last person that you would want to deal with. The idea of conversing on a philosophical level with your dead grandmother would seem more appropriate.

It was then that the thought first occurred to me that maybe Jacob wasn't ready for any kind of a mind-meltdown. No one truly is, but especially not him. "There was no use in arguing this though," I thought. I was confident that I would never get my point across to Hess. I could tell that he had conspired to initiate Jacob into our psychedelic club without me. Whether I believed that he was ready or not was inconsequential now; the experience had been put into motion already.

Besides, I can't say that I wasn't curious myself as to how the night would unfold. Witnessing someone's first trip was almost equivalent to going into space.

Our night had been planned. Everything was in order. We expected no trouble. I was to drop Hess off at his house where he would meet Helen and Lena. Jacob and I were to get the acid from Chris. Later, we would all gather at the pond.

DROP

CHAPTER 3

A Heart Tattered and a Soul Weakened

Jacob was the quiet type of person. He kept his thoughts to himself, and one could tell that his thoughts troubled him. Even when he smiled or laughed there was something sorrowing his eyes. It was always there. Maybe to someone that didn't know him it would seem he was just shy because of his stand-offish character, but I knew it was something deeper and more troubling.

It seeded from the loss of his mother.

It only took a little more than a year for her to shrivel painfully to almost nothing more than a frail coat of skin hardly pigmented hugging disintegrating bones. Her bedroom had become more of a tomb than anything else, smelling of her ensuing death more and more each day. She was unable to function in any sensible day to day life, so Sheriff Kahn stayed home every day to care for her. The rich and noisome aroma of her room conjured tears every time he stepped into it, but he managed because she needed him.

His deep and unconditional love resonated within Jacob. Even at a young age he helped care for her, not as a duty, but out of love by performing small, but important tasks. He would bring her crushed chips of ice to rub on her dry and chapped lips, or for her to suck because the unrelenting pain in her stomach wouldn't allow much more inside. Sometimes he would rub ointment on the fleshy sores that bubbled upon her skin as she winced from the pain. He would lay cool and dampened rags on her face because it always seemed to be intensely burning as she sweated more and more. Mostly though, it was his reading that would calm her pain. Even when it was ascending on her and twisting within her rotting loins like mating pythons, seeping pure agony throughout, when he read any of his Dr. Seuss stories to her the hurt wrenching her withered face departed and was replaced by something close to content. Their favorite was one titled: Red Fish Blue Fish One Fish Two Fish – to which he would sing the rhymes adorably in his innocent childish voice.

She died, in grave pain, in the solemn fortitude of night while Jacob slept in his room. That scarred morning, when he awoke, he found several men shuffling anxiously like unwelcomed ghosts in his home. Before whatever lingering dreams from the night could dissipate completely from his slowly waking mind he saw his father at the dinner table with his head bowed and sobbing.

Clutching the Dr. Seuss book in his hands, he slowly walked down the hall. The stench of her sickness grew louder the further he walked. The door to the bedroom was cracked. The stench of fresh death crept from it like an invisible shadow. He peeked, boldly, through the tiny crack hoping like hell to see his mother lying awake and smiling, but he knew within himself somehow that she was gone. He saw the empty chair where he sat singing the words to his favorite stories while kicking his feet with excitement by the bed as his mother listened, in a sweeter kind of pain. It was now also empty, only remnants of her bleeding sores stained the sheets of her bed where she had laid.

He dropped the book and ran to his room.

He wept uncontrollably and refused to speak for seven weeks after that painful morning.

If only he could've sung one last story.

.....

I glanced at Jacob in my rearview mirror as I drove. Hess was telling of some crazed conspiracy he had concocted, but I could see that he was somewhere else. Perhaps the ghost of his mother haunted his thoughts continuously, I couldn't know.

I was somewhat concerned how the acid would react with him. This too, I couldn't know, at least until the time arrived.

"Are you listening to me, bro?" Hess asked with a demanding sort of tone.

My concentration snapped, my reverie of Jacob's pain distracted by Hess' interruption.

"Just hear me out," he continued, "I'm serious about this."

"Okay. Yes! I'm listening!"

Among all of Hess' unique qualities as a deranged person, he was obsessed with conspiracies. I can't say that they were all legitimate, but some were rather clever, and a few were probably true.

He began with his newest theory – probably born to him in the haze of marijuana smoke just minutes prior. I glanced at Jacob just to see if he was listening. He was staring out the window, his thoughts adrift.

"This just shows how the government can control everything, man. How those greedy, sneaky bastards always find a way to get all they can."

"Just get to the point, man," I demanded. "And pass that joint before it goes out."

He continued, "the Pentecostal Church, dude. They fucking infiltrated it. Check it out. Think about it. From the beginning, it was Holiness and just Pentecostal branches of the church, right? These people only wore, like, long - ass dresses, no make-up at all, and kept their hair plain – cutting it themselves. That was the women, obviously. The men, were basically the same, wearing long-sleeved shirts and pants – not much else. They didn't buy shit, ever – only the necessities. They don't watch tv and the only books they read are either the Bible or something related to it. There's no way that the government could ever capitalize on them. Suddenly, certain preachers all over the country began popping up and telling these people that it's okay to be fashionable and flamboyant, as long as they kept the Holy Spirit in them. The Assembly of God churches started sprouting everywhere. All they did was keep the same crazy beliefs where they fall out and speak tongues, or what-not. Then there's all this shitty Contemporary Christian music, suddenly, popping up out of nowhere. Music where all they do is rip off secular music and add Christian lyrics. Keep in mind everything secular is the devil to the old-school Pentecostal folks. They even rip off fashion trends and copyrighted t-shirt slogans and make it Christian to sell in their churches."

I sighed, rolled my eyes as I passed him the joint, "dude, what in the hell is your point?"

He got emphatic and raised his hand as if he were going to hit me. "It's the fucking government, man. Don't you see? They weren't profiting enough off the old-school crazies, so they planted phony preachers everywhere and started the Assembly of God movement to raise their profit. It's all consumerism man."

I could tell in his tone and see the glimmer in his eyes that he believed this entirely. No point in arguing, I thought.

"Very interesting, man," I said.

"Damn right. Fucking government," he said. "Same thing is happening right now with the whole goth scene."

I snorted in laughter, "what?"

"Hell yeah. Haven't you noticed how slowly it's getting more commercial. Five years ago, goths were all about anti-commercialism. That's what was up with all the black and shit – it was symbolic of separating themselves from the mainstream. Now this whole emo thing is rising and it started with the music - while adopting the goth look. They just blend more materialism, hence the colored hair and stylistic clothing. Watch what I say, ten years from now this emo stuff will have taken over. Thanks to the government's infiltration of music and media."

I laughed, his theory was preposterous and he was an asshole. "So basically, the goths are the Pentecostals and the Emos are the Assembly of God?"

"Exactly."

I peeked at Jacob again in the rearview. He was smiling, but I could tell apprehension rendered his emotions. There was that same stare he had - one of longing and permanent loss. I understood this as being from his mother and the lost opportunity to sing the last story.

But now it was different. It was fear that I sensed.

He looked up and noticed me staring at him. "What is it?" He asked barely smiling, now.

"Nothing, man. Nothing."

CHAPTER 4

Chimes of Madness Ring

Chris was a short, chubby, and wiry-haired friend of mine. He had eyes like Charles Manson's which were wide, deep, and penetrating – being one of the many signs indicating that he reeked of insanity. If a sketch artist for some reason had to draw him the finished product would resemble, incredibly, a modern composite of Ludwig Van Beethoven. No matter the occasion he seemed to always be bare-footed or wearing worn-out sandals with no socks. His lazy attire and drudgingly un-kempt facial hair made him resemble something like a fat Jesus; because with no doubt if Jesus had been a fat stoner he would have been Chris.

Chris also had strange tics which made people around him very nervous. Tics, such as pacing calmly from room to room murmuring to himself balefully as if it were all perfectly normal. Sometimes he would just stare blindly into nothing without blinking or breaking his gaze for several minutes at a time. Nevertheless, it was his eccentric rarity and abrasive needlessness to attract that paradoxically attracted me to him; or perhaps we were both essentially the same breed of psychotic creatures.

Regardless of all things philosophical and psychological, Chris was indeed his own rare specimen of spontaneous and common indecency. Often, I would wonder quietly to myself if maybe he were an endangered mutant of some particular kind, only known of, but never spoken about, among elite genealogical circles.

He was undoubtedly too weird and rare; uncommon to anything social. We repeatedly worked ourselves into sordid drug-induced types of frenzies, and even then, he always seemed out of place and unpredictable, like a castrated porn star balefully lingering around an orgy. He possessed an uncanny ability to make everyone around him feel uncomfortable. It was his obtuseness that I embraced as a friend and admired as an avid spectator and fiend for the strange which he perfected.

Jacob and I arrived at his house twenty minutes after leaving Hess at his house. It had been a quiet ride, exceedingly different from when Hess was around. I was eager to score the LSD, but I had the unction that Jacob was a bit apprehensive. He had been sitting quietly in the passenger seat the entire ride, then as if to prove me correct he asked, "so you're not afraid of having a bad trip?"

It was a question I had never really entertained. I considered it to be more of a myth than reality, therefore, wrote it off as improbable. As for Jacob, I could sense this possibility disconcerted his view of our whole night. Jacob had lived a simple life. He was smart and somewhat withdrawn from the invaluable oddities of the world. There was also the fact that his father was the town sheriff.

There was also the question of what was considered bad?

I could sense his fear building and warned him that it was not in his or my best interest to worry or be afraid just before his first time. He stared ahead behind those thick, comical glasses that he always wore. His frail, skinny bodily frame was posed in the seat like a skeleton smoking a cigarette. I could see that he was nervous about our endeavor, for he had heard the same tales growing up as I had. The main difference, of course, was that his father was a cop, so the propaganda against hallucinogenic drugs was probably much more intense.

I knew that I had to ease his thoughts. If I didn't, who could tell, he may be chewing the face off an elderly woman in a few hours.

Fear will discomfit any rational agenda; especially when LSD is involved.

"You can't think like that, man," I said considerately, halfway believing it myself.

He seemed to heed my wisdom. After all, I had become something of an expert on the matter, why wouldn't he?

I parked in Chris' yard. The grass was high, and limbs from the looming oak tree lay scattered like debris left by a storm in the yard. His house, he rented for probably close to nothing, was barely standing. Its wood was painted white but had chipped and peeled away long ago. It was a sad and dilapidated sight. There were cinder blocks stacked upon each other that served as steps to the rickety porch invaded by cobwebs and dirt dauber nests.

I knocked on his door and then waited long enough to realize that he wasn't going to come and open it. Jacob was beside me, like a stone in his composure. Worry gripped his stare and it seemed that a pallid hue began to flush over him. This would pass I told myself and gave him a reassuring wink and nod before letting myself inside.

Instantly, upon entering, we both gagged from some acrid and evil stench. I had never smelled a dead hippy before but was sure that I was smelling one at that moment.

We moved slowly through the dirty kitchen, both of us barely able to breathe from the pungency of the odor. It seemed to have its own soul and had itself died some time ago, ripening perfectly for the moment that we entered. With my shirt over my face and Jacob mimicking me so that only our eyes were visible we entered the drab living room. The curtains were drawn over the windows and the lights were off, expectedly. Cigarette smoke swam through the closed off air, hovering above us like an evil entity poised to pounce on us. The television was on, a young woman screamed just before she was knocked to the ground in the woods and some possessed vine scurried up her skirt. Insane horror films had become a regular experience in this place making it difficult to relax at all at times.

Chris sat on his couch, his jaws clenched shut like he was having a seizure and his eyes were wider than usual as he watched the ants work tirelessly behind the glass of his ant farm. It was propped directly in front of him on the table before his couch. I could see by the absent gaze and frozen dead-like calmness of his features that he was in the later stages of his trip, just after the stormy peak ends and your mind is left reeling after the effects.

"Holy Manson," I belched while lighting a joint, "you're completely fucking sideways aren't you man."

He muttered something, perhaps even something prolific, but I'll never know what because only he knew. To me it sounded like, "forty-six and two."

Jacob took a seat on the couch next to him and took the joint from my hand. Chris never looked away from the ant farm as I picked up a Visine bottle from beside it on the table. I held it to the pale glow of the television, where a woman's severed head was clinched in a vice as she spat obscenities in a possessed tone at a chainsaw-wielding man. A stinging chill swam over my skin. I perused it as if it were some alien artifact. It was possible that my eyes were deceiving me in the dark and gloomy habitat, but it appeared that the bottle contained an ominous black concoction.

"What the hell is this, man?" I asked over the buzz of a chainsaw splitting the woman's skull.

"Can't you see? It's terrific." He replied with the monotonous slur of a librarian on Xanax.

For a moment, I was in disbelief. Could this have been the acid that I had come to purchase? Or had my friend's mind finally fully deteriorated into madness?

"But its black," I said dubiously.

In the dark room, lit by only by the glow of horror from the television, smoke trailed up from the cigarette stuck between his lips and he said again in the same trance-like tone, "it's terrific."

He then blinked slowly. The zombie expression and serene contentment in his voice forced me to believe him. Chris was many uncouthly things (a fiendish ghoul, a mad man on dope, even a hell of a listener when needed), but a liar was not one of them.

"It works better if you drop it in your eye," he said while still gazing at the ants. His voice sang the words like a mother crooning an infant. I wondered if he even meant to do it or if the black liquid had completely desecrated his mind to the desperate point where now he spoke only in song. This apparently caught Jacob's attention because now he watched Chris out of the corner of his eye like someone might a known pervert hanging around a kid's park. He continued in a weakened tone, "it's better to drop it in your eye."

Regardless if he was speaking from a dislocated mind, I believed him. And why not? It seemed perfectly logical. Even if logic had completely deteriorated somehow in the dense haze of marijuana and cigarette smoke slowly shrinking his living room, it was still in a way logic; and logic is what separates men from stupid, wild beasts. And as far as my logic could ascertain at that point we had not become beasts just yet.

I tilted my head back and raised the bottle up. Speaking over the crazed, demonic giggles escaping the television I said, "well, if you insist man." Mockingly reassuring myself I continued, "I mean why the fuck not, right? No point in dragging this thing out."

Although the drug looked as if it could've been witch piss, I squeezed two heavy drops into each of my eyes anyway. I squinted to reduce the burn and passed the Visine bottle to Jacob, who was still on the couch. The awful smell we encountered when we first entered the house hit me again and suddenly I felt as if I were going to puke. I had forgotten about the smell when we came into the living room. Perhaps, instead of it being because of my mind getting used to the pungency, it was that I had walked into an uncontrolled asylum, where lunacy and reason quarreled with reality, that I had ignored it. I covered my mouth to catch the vomit just in case, but none came. Jacob took the bottle from my fingers slowly as confusion and worry contorted his face. Who could blame him for being a little freaked out? After all, he had never been around anyone tripping before and now he sat beside someone such as Chris, a madman singing uncouthly.

I suddenly felt that it was a bad idea to have brought him.

"I don't have to put that shit in my eye, right?" He asked me with a timid whisper as if he didn't want the maniac beside him to hear.

I also didn't want him to hear. I don't know why, only that slowly a certain sense of dread began to palpitate within me and I then began to have a strong desire to run out of there. A ridiculous and absurd thought ripped through me like the sting of a shot that perhaps it was the enchantment of the LSD, which was already permeating the environment, that was so potent and effective it's mere presence in the bottle was powerful enough to affect the mind – much like that damned ring from the Tolkien books. After all, it couldn't be denied, by myself at least, that I had sensed its evil when I first felt the bottle.

Or had I? I couldn't remember.

Was it casting some devious spell on me now? Already?

No. Certainly, that is illogical.

I shook my head, telling Jacob he didn't have to while stealing a glance at Chris. His wide, starry eyes opened even more-so, and his jaws unclenched. It was too late. Our attempt to sneak past the hound had failed. He had heard Jacob and responded with true maniacal elegance. A frozen smile etched across his face like a fleshless skull, and without blinking, he simply sang in no particular tone, "You could just cut open your wrists and pour the magic into your veins."

The torn mask of sanity that had been frailly covering Chris' face during the visit had now been violently peeled back. Now, discernable traces of delirium and skewed psychosis were carving their permanent mark on his soul right before my eyes. He screeched with a sort of terrifying hilarity from someplace deep within his twisted maw. He rocked his upper body back and forth like a confused pendulum, blending it with a horrible laughter that mimicked some crazed witch from a classic cartoon. He howled louder with fervid, pure madness while never once blinking his eyes as he stared into an unseen oblivion. The environment had quickly become unfathomably insane.

I wanted to snatch Jacob up from the couch and protect him as if he were a child and stop him from ingesting the menace before it was too late. It was only a tangible feeling that I had, unexplainable in fact, but real. Besides, the demonic laughter spewing out of Chris like vomit from a baby and the carrion-like stench was a bad omen. Egregious things would happen to me now, I just knew it. And there wasn't a damn thing I could do to stop it. There was no hope for me now, the acid was already seeping into my bloodstream and preparing to shred my senses with feline-like claws. It was only a matter of time before I was doing unspeakable acts as some alien entity tools the machine inside me.

Yes, I had wanted to save Jacob, but it was too late for him now as well. Before I could tackle him to the ground and jar the bottle from his grasp he dropped the poison on his tongue.

Within myself I heard an unfamiliar laughter.

As Chris fondled at the skirt of insanity, still laughing wildly, I bolted for the door in nothing short of a panic. Jacob followed close behind, puzzled and confused yet eager to vanquish the lair as well. We left the mad man to his cigarette smoke and looming hysteria; not to mention the crude stench getting louder by every second that we had stayed. We couldn't get to the truck fast enough. The strange occurrence had left me confused and unable to distinguish between being fucked up and being fucking insane.

Jacob spoke aloud as I hardly listened. He talked of a bad trip and of feeling afraid inside. Though I could concur, I dared not to.

As I drove, I mulled the encounter over and over in my head. I found myself wondering, again, about the smothering sense of panic that swelled inside of me while in that room. It wasn't the first time I found myself questioning the mental status of my friend Chris, but I had never felt that kind of uneasiness.

Could the catalyst of all that fear and inner turmoil paralyzing me have been the demon-spit in that Visine bottle?

Could it have been powerful enough to radiate its potential to me from within? I had felt the dread, I was sure.

Could it have been just Chris' inept character freaking me out – formulating scandalous vibes for me to intake?

Or was it just me freaking out?

These questions plagued me, but the only thing certain is that I had very little time before I possibly became a deranged, howling zombie. This possibility was genuine and resurrected the same essential question I couldn't shake: had Chris inconveniently dabbled in lunacy for a short trip? Or had he completely lost his shit this time?

What would happen now?

As I pondered this intriguing concept I could hear Jacob babbling something about Chris belonging in a zoo. My mind projected him completely twisted on acid in a cage, laughing vigorously, with fellow monkeys as they sat together huddled in groups picking lice from one another. The image appeased my anxious mind a bit and allowed me to relax; if only sort of.

I continued to try not to worry myself as I drove. Worry led to fear; and fear, under the influence of a potent chemical hallucinogen, led to hellish and freakish encounters with unchartered parts of the mind that you never want to fuck with. These are just facts. Simple things learned on the fly and not taught in classrooms – though they should be. Facts such as these could save some poor asshole from clawing off his own face in a mirror.

I knew that we were both in for a trip. This, too, was a fact. This was certain and quickly approaching. I thought that I was ready. I hoped that Jacob was ready. I had him play Tool's 'Eulogy' to relax us further. I was mindful not to suggest anything to harm the frailty of his mind, for our trip was only beginning.

DROP

CHAPTER 5

Inception

A warm, tingling wave passed over and through me as I drifted down the highway. The light of the moon painted what resembled furry faces in the treetops as I passed. My headlights drowned out the night in front of me. I knew there was no turning back now. I drove onward, cutting through the darkness further into the unknown.

Was anything for sure or did chaos reign indefinitely? Was life left to suffer a series of hopeless chances?

This could be true, unless of course there are various jealous and vengeful gods somewhere assigned to every aspect of life as we know it, such as how the ancient Greeks believed. These immortals were apt to covertly meddle with our mortal fates while creating a wonderful fallacy of chance and chaos.

Maybe, among the great sons of Cronos, there was one forgotten; a lost immortal brother of Zeus, Poseidon, and Hades who wanders aimlessly in an altered realm where he greedily receives our senses as sacrifices as we lose them to hallucinogenic drugs.

Who is to say there is not a god of hallucination, stumbling around in some other realm getting his rocks off with strange and unusual interventions for those of us under the influence?

All of this seems perfectly reasonable if you are somewhat mad, like me; it explains events in my life that are incidentally unexplainable. I never could exempt the possibility of this theory, nor the probability that I was the first to have examined his existence, therefore it shall only be right that I name him. The most fitting title for him that I can think of is Azzore. There is no particular reason for this name, only that I think it sounds cool; and besides I was the first to name him, so I can call him anything I damn well please.

A part of me wants to believe that some immortal being with pull in how things work in the universal scheme manipulates and sets forth into motion some cosmic intervention disguised as chance. All, of course, to just to toy with us. This is a strange and ridiculous notion, I know, but when you have seen insanely horrible things like a kid with Down Syndrome who, also, was a raging homosexual while on acid you must ask questions. Questions like: How is this even possible? Or, Jesus, God really had it out for this kid's parents, didn't He? Due to mind-blowing things such as this that seem to only occur when under the influence of some hallucinogen makes me look back and wonder if it is all possible because of mere chance? Or is it more plausible to assume some cosmic manipulation occurred to have put me in the moment?

I found myself thinking of the first time that Hess tripped. It was with me, of course, and remains to this day a strong example of persuasion unto the belief of cosmic intervention; while tripping at least.

.....

Usually while tripping the bizarre and psychotic hallucinations that deceive your mind are indeed fallacies brought about by a fracture from your sense and reality, but sometimes inept situations arise that make you sincerely question the seriousness of that reality.

Once, while significantly puddled out, Hess and I stopped at a random store off the highway that was blinking with a fantastic array of colors. I had felt compelled to grab orange juice for myself, and though he somewhat contested it, a laser light for Hess. The laser light was essential for no good reason, but it was always better to be prepared than not.

Sadly, Hess was too far gone to go inside – there was no way I could truly trust him around strangers, for you never know how these things can go - so I left him to the safe confinement of my car. Bravely, but confused and greatly disoriented, I shambled like a drunk mummy towards the entrance of the store. From somewhere in the parking lot I heard music playing, but I paid it no mind, for a zinging sting of paranoia penetrated me as I suddenly realized that the door of entry was hidden somewhere among a sparkling wall of glass windows. Everything before me was clean and clear, reflecting the brilliant lights screaming behind me and making a shimmery glaze of transparency that was impossible to penetrate.

I thought that I was sure there was a door leading inside, but I couldn't find it. I pushed on what I thought was it, but the glass was impregnable. Everywhere I tried was impervious to my force. I tapped and slapped with my hands at the slick surface, but nothing seemed to work. Perhaps then, I thought, I should pull. I felt around like a blind man in a funhouse, high and low on the glass, but there was nothing to grab. I carefully walked further down, keeping, my hands skimming along the glass, but failed to find any way inside still. I was beginning to think that some cruel and bastard trick was being played on me. Perhaps, maybe, if I waited patiently some charismatic man leading a camera crew with a microphone and a great hair-cut would come and put an end to this nightmare.

I gasped thankfully as I heard a bell ding very close to me and a door swing open. An elderly woman clutching a carton of cigarettes and a twelve pack of Pabst Blue Ribbon under her wrinkly arm stepped out into the glow of the blinking lights in the night. I scampered past her, hurrying to catch the door before it closed and was lost forever. I mumbled a polite thank you, even as she poked at me with a rude and blasphemous stare.

Inside I could see that others were staring in awe of me. Their curious gazes gave me the unshakable feeling that I was, to them, some caged mutant finally set free in an unfamiliar environment. There was an entire family of approximately eight Hispanics ranging from different ages and genders. A hint of dread cradled me when I noticed that every one of them had a thick, bushy unibrow stuck like a caterpillar above their eyes. Even the fucking baby in a stroller had one, for Christ's sake. They all peered at me blandly and when they blinked it was with incredible synchronicity as if they were all functioning as one unit together.

Behind the counter was a middle-aged black man who politely nodded at me as if he were unsure of what else to do.

I spoke boldly and clearly, I think, for I didn't want to seem as if certainty was tainted. "I just need orange juice and a laser for my friend. He's in the car."

I'm quite sure that the Hispanic family didn't understand what was happening. They only stood there, blinking together under their massive eyebrows, which incidentally made my mind kink as the trip sped up. The father collected his change and his kids, corralling them past me and out of the door.

From here everything went smoothly, inside the store at least. The black man behind the counter, who I am positive sympathized with my affliction, helped me by grabbing the things that I needed as

I followed him around witlessly. After I managed to give him money and received my change he even went so far as leaving the counter again just to open the door for me. He laughed hysterically as he did it, advising me to be careful.

Instantly, after walking outside I heard the music again. It wept like an unseen siren from the shore of a forlorn island and the unknown origin of it began to drive me mad. My poor mind began to fixate on the mystery. It was much too loud to be coming from any neighboring businesses, I thought, for it was almost as if it were being played directly in my head.

What kind of forsaken place was this that emitted music freely from mysterious bunkers in the night?

And just who in God's great motherfuck of a world even listens to George Michael anymore?

I was befuddled by both the blatant secrecy and poor taste. I found that I was getting more than a bit vexed that some sneaky bastard would go to such great lengths to hide and blast crappy music in my general direction. As I trudged through the parking lot he was probably getting his proverbial rocks off at my perplexed countenance.

I walked to my car, cursing the evil bastard that hid from me, and pulled on the handle to open the door, but it didn't work. With everything else that had gone awry, maybe it shouldn't have surprised me at this point that my car door refused to function correctly, but it did. I pulled at it again, this time much harder, and still it didn't open.

"Hess unlock the damn door, man." I said looking around nervously, "some cheeky bastard is out here and he's playing George Michael. For the love of the Lizard King, man, hurry."

I waited a moment for the click of the latch, but it never came. Severe sensations of anxiousness and paranoia ensued. I thought that breaking the glass would be my best option for a moment but convinced myself that I was in no shape for breaking things. I had to come up with a plan. Hess was most likely in the chilly grip of a tranquil descent into somewhere pleasant, or he had fallen asleep. Either way he wasn't going to open the door for me, I thought. I began to fish for my keys in my pockets clumsily, flinging bits of loose change onto the gravel of the parking lot, but they weren't there. Naturally, I assumed that I was just high and so I double checked, drastically making a show of it as I ravaged my pants pockets.

Creeping Jesus, I thought. What is this?

What's next?

The music then changed to Abba. My senses gave way to inadequacy.

Was nothing sane any longer?

A drenching flood of confusion and muddling thoughts that bore no relevance to reason drowned my mind. I pulled on the door handle again, several times; desperately hoping that I had been mistaken in thinking that it was locked. I began mumbling out loud incoherently, even to myself, trying to unravel sense where there was none.

Suddenly, sense hit me like some divine word. I knelt and looked inside the car through the glass and just as I suspected Hess wasn't there. It was obvious, now, that he was in on it – that the bastards had gotten to him. Somehow, he had slipped the keys without me knowing and possibly even changed the locks. Now he was hiding somewhere watching me and chuckling with a boom-box blasting shitty music from the corner of darkness out there beyond me.

I looked around frantically, not at all liking my predicament, and I remember thinking that this is no time for a game of hide and seek.

It was then that from the picturesque black abyss beyond the parking lot that a blinding pair of headlights coming towards me, froze me where I stood. The car slugged closer to me and parked directly beside my car. I couldn't believe what I was seeing though. The car was the same as mine. It was the same skeleton gray with silver trim. The tone of the color was ugly and unmistakable, resembling something that an alien would cough up. It was the same make, a 1992 Nissan Sentra. Even the tires and rims were the same.

I took a step back to be sure if indeed I was seeing what I believed to be seeing. Sometimes, instances of double vision became symptoms of the mind while in the throes of a trip such as the one I was currently on. In all seriousness, and to be fair, it was entirely possible that my mind was only echoing what my eyes had seen and that the image of the car parked beside mine was a projected mirror. It was then, as I was contemplating all feasible realms of probabilities that a familiar looking elderly woman erupted from the driver's seat of the car and began apologizing to me cryptically in a ravenous sort of fashion. This strange and unforeseen encounter frightened and shook my sticky senses free from my conscious. I could feel my face tighten into a frozen yawn as I silently recoiled.

My mind stuttered for answers.

Who was this crazed woman reeking of alcohol and what did she want?

More importantly, who was I to her and what had she done to me?

She lunged closer with her hands out apologetically, and I fell back shrieking, "what the fuck do you mean?"

She was babbling now, or at least I perceived her to be. Perhaps my defensive nature had given her a slight nudge over the edge, I thought. Her words had become a sloppy mixture of apologies and explanation. She would pause only to take long yanks from a cigarette and then go right back to her performance.

Although my mind was fretted by the drug I began to string together the meaning of her apology. First, I recognized the old woman as being the same person that exited the store as I entered just minutes before. It was her tough, leathery, wrinkled skin that had undoubtedly seen too much sun that was apparently familiar to me. Secondly, it was evident that I was correct in thinking that she had a car exactly like mine, only it wasn't her car she had lunged out from after nearly causing my brain to convulse in frenzied tantrums – it was my car. This was clear to me because, thirdly, I spotted Hess lying where I had left him in the passenger seat through the driver's door she left open.

I used my ability to establish plausible scenarios by means of deductive reasoning to ascertain that in a reasonably understandable, yet highly unlikely, misunderstanding the confused old woman with booze and smokes in her hands jumped into my car thinking it was hers. Apparently, she had failed to notice the strange, enhancing, music or the enhanced young man reclined in the passenger seat. I can only imagine the wild and hysterical performance she must've given when she did realize her folly.

When she was nearly finished apologizing I saw fit that I should at least say something. I remembered the bastardly stare she had given me as we passed at the entrance door, so by driving condemnation deep in my tone I said, "you're fucking right you're sorry, man! What were you thinking? You should be ashamed of yourself dammit!"

She could only stare at me with disbelieving eyes. She had no idea how to cope emotionally after realizing that I may have been completely mad. I scoffed disappointingly and hurried past her, smelling the booze on her breath.

In my car, I found Hess, complacent as always, with his face turned to the night outside his window. Radiohead's 'Paranoid Android' was softly vibrating the air within. I finally felt at ease again as I coasted onto the highway and dove into the night, leaving the old drunk lady alone by her car. The fact that I wasn't, after all, being spied upon by some deviant with an endless selection of horrible music to torment me with greatly soothed my tension.

Once the initial euphoria of Radiohead had worn off a bit I asked, "how far did you guys get, man?" When he didn't answer I waited several seconds before asking again. He still didn't reply. The fancifully morbid, yet realistic enough, thought pounced on my mind that maybe the old hag had cut his throat and was now pinning his murder on me. After all, who in their right mind would ever believe some old drunk lady stole my car and bled my best friend out in the matter of only minutes. I was done for.

I had been caught red-handed, although I never did a damn thing but want orange juice and a laser light.

I shook him violently with my free hand and shouted, "fucker!"

He bewilderedly, yet lethargically, opened his eyes and swam them all around, "what the hell, dude?"

"I said how far did you get, man?"

"How far what? What the piss are you saying right now, dude?"

"Damn it, you bastard! How far did the old woman and you get before turning around?"

Hess blinked once, maybe twice, and looked at me as if I had just jerked my own brain through one of my nostrils with a pair of forceps and said, "dude, what fucking lady?"

.....

I was still driving as these memories and thoughts were spilling from my brain. Though I had control of the wheel, it felt as if my head believed my body was somewhere outside bathing in the wind. I loved driving in this heightened conditioned. My senses were tuned in on every minute detail around me; the traffic lights glowing red or green casting their painted shadows on the road below, catching broken glass giving the beautiful mirage of rubies and emeralds scattered in pools. The wind blowing through my window and down my shirt then through my hair smelled like the clouds I had never touched. There is nothing better than feeling the motion from within you as your favorite song swims in your body while hearing it.

I was somewhere between purgatory and heaven, that first gear of the trip that never grinded and always seemed to go smooth, when I heard Jacob beside me say, "oh no. Check this out man."

I glanced over and at first couldn't tell what he was holding in his hand, but then the light from outside somewhat flashed through the window for a brief second and I saw it. The bottle holding that foul stuff rested in his palm like a venomous snake. The black potion blended in with the night perfectly and gave me a shudder.

"Fucking hell man!" I exclaimed, "where did that come from?"

Jacob stared at me, not confused, but still suffering while trying to think. I could see that he too had begun his journey and his mind was catching up. He didn't have to say it, I knew what had happened. We both had left in such a hurry because of Chris' insensate behavior that he had merely forgotten to put the bottle back on the table. It was a simple mistake that could be fixed, just not tonight. Going back to that harbor for insanity in our state at this moment would be disastrous, to say the least. Besides, who knew what lucid psychotic state Chris had delved into by now.

I took it from him and put it in my ashtray, closing it so that its presence wouldn't infiltrate my well-being. It was strange how it made me feel just by being in my sight. I feared it was cursed in some way, spreading forth its power.

But that was crazy, right?

I had to stop at the Quick and Go for rolling papers and orange juice. The brightly lit parking lot pierced my eyes like the head of a sharp needle, giving my mind a slight and painful jerk. The climate was mild and the air seemed clean enough. The lot was empty, which was good because people didn't like me when I was slipping from reality; or maybe it was the other way; either way is correct, I assume.

I walked inside, and the wailing of a sad man in a country song played from a radio somewhere, then I immediately forgot what I was to get. I wondered around seeming lost, content with nothing, everything that I saw was all wrong. Already, I noticed that the woman behind the counter had seen me. I felt the desire to hide, but in this place, there was nowhere — mirrors everywhere, copying my every move.

Just as I expected that it would, it got worse. All at once, on the floor, the square tiles began to bend upward and roll with tumultuous waves that seemed to be breathing the air in deep gasps beneath my feet. I sincerely felt that I was going to tip over and be lost forever. I straddled my legs for balance and out-stretched my arms for better support as the waves swayed beneath me. I walked in this silly manner as if I were balancing on a tight rope, for quite a while when I saw the clerk again – this time eyeing me as if I were a crazed pedophile high on crack trying to lift a school bus and run away with it.

Now, paranoia rumbled through me and crackled in my nerves because I knew now that she knew I was tripping. Perhaps the most peculiar part is that I knew what I was doing and couldn't stop myself; because the damn floor was melting and shaking. It was as if I were dreaming and couldn't wake up, or drowning while trying to breathe the water. A better analogy would be that it was as if I were burning alive, but still trying hold a polite conversation. After some time of rigorous meditation, I was able to find my footing, and the orange juice, then myself while standing awkwardly like a failed martyr in front of the woman at the counter.

I was spent, tired and confused.

Intolerable paranoia paralyzed me and itched my every fiber. The clerk peered at me, seeming to try and figure me out as if I were an alien on exhibit. I forgot what I was doing again, and I was both sweating and salivating profusely like a retarded child excited on a roller coaster. Right then my mind deformed to mush and I could actually feel it happening in the back crevices of my eyes. I stared at her blankly waiting to recall what to do next; even my thoughts mumbled, so I dared to not utter a word aloud. The woman opened her mouth to speak but instead a bird chirped sharply and above me a baby laughed. I jumped back in surprise nearly dropping my jug of orange juice.

"What the fuck is that?" I mumbled. "What?"

"Is that all?" She said, apparently not noticing my little tantrum within my conscious. I sensed that she eagerly wanted me out of her store. And who could blame her? Jesus, three minutes prior I could barely stand or walk because the floor was pretending to boil and melt at my feet. Now I stood in front of her sweaty, salivating, pale, and holding juice.

All I could do was nod, although I knew that wasn't all that I needed. There was most definitely something else, I was sure of this, but I would've been Jeffrey Dahmer's zombie-lover before speaking up at a horrible moment such as this. All I knew was that I had to get out of there. The walls were closing in. The bastards were coming.

But what bastards?

I didn't know — all of them I supposed.

I managed to give her some money and take my change. I kept my head down and hurried out without mumbling anything else, for I knew that she knew something was amiss, just as I did; and that evil bitch was most likely in on it.

I stepped out into the young night. My hands and face were tingling because of the dark substance drowning my brain, making it bleed. I was relieved to be rid of that horrible woman's stare and out of that store. It was no place for a person in my condition.

As I got into my car, I said something like, "Jesus man! I forgot the papers!" Which I had, but there was a better chance of me spontaneously combusting before going back in there, for I knew what awaited.

Jacob didn't respond, only stared at the sky silently.

I already had the car in reverse and was very slowly backing up when a fist beat on my window causing me to jump violently and thrash the brake pedal suddenly.

"David fucking Berkowitz, man!" I exclaimed with my heart racing. I glanced at Jacob who seemed not even to notice the severity of the disturbance. He still sat motionless watching nothing; the acid had him bogged between that first and second gripping gear.

I heard annoying laughter coming from outside, and although the mood for me wasn't there yet, I let my window down.

Mark and Murray stood at my door, both laughing. They were each racially challenged so they wore baggy pants hanging lazily off their asses and shirts a size or two too large. They were equipped with gold chains to finish out the apparel.

The acid was raging strong, and my adrenaline had just been jacked, so when I spoke, it was more of a yell. "What the fuck do you want, dammit!"

With some rehearsed form of stylish linguistic communication Murray said, "what up playa? Who's wit ya? Ahh, Jacob! What up son?"

His arrogant and thuggish countenance frustrated me greatly because I knew it to be fake, for he didn't always speak like this – especially around adults.

"Absolutely not shit, man," I said trying not to make eye contact. I did not care for these assholes, they made me nervous and jittery, and I wanted to leave.

"Damn, what up with all dat OJ?" Mark inquired peering inside my car. He had gold teeth in his front, and they sparkled under the exuberant show of lights in the parking lot as he spoke. For a moment, I thought he might cough fire.

"To drink," I said matter-of-factly. "Now I need to leave, man." It was a true statement because itchy, grasping vibes began to cling to me.

They exchanged glances at one another and quickly directed their attention back to me. "Y'all is trippin' ain't ya," Mark said, "hell yeah. Look at Jacob sittin' over there all fucked up." They both began to giggle.

"No, we're not," I scoffed. "Now leave us be you pesky fucking bastards!"

They insisted on me telling them where to get some and wouldn't have let me go if I kept it from them. I knew I had practically a whole bottle in my ashtray, but to hell with these guys, I thought. They didn't earn their trip as I had. Let them, too, face the mad beast in his dooming lair and get it for themselves. I sure he had more of the rotten stuff lying around, and even if he didn't that was fine with me.

"Chris!" I yelled, still not able to control the volume of voice to a rational tone, the acid had switched gears with me, and I was cruising in second – the altered perception of everything phase. "Just walk inside," I continued, "he's home now and has all you will ever need."

"Chris? Crazy Chris?" Murray said disappointedly. "I hate that freak. But okay. Thanks, B."

"Be sure to tell him I sent you," I shouted as I backed up and began to leave.

The two of them raced to Murray's car and threw me some foolish hand gesture I couldn't fully understand but could assume meant 'bye'.

Through the whole strenuous ordeal, I'm not sure if Jacob even moved. He still had that dull stare which let me know that his gear was different, or even stickier, than mine. I was paranoid and somewhat delusional, but for the most part, functioning quite well. He seemed, on the surface, to be in a calm and passive bodily state, yet his eyes spoke to me, and they said with stunning clarity that inside he was roiling and ready to explode.

Despite the catatonic-like rage hidden behind his forlorn stare he turned to me, and with the voice of a sane and serious man said, without ever looking away from my eyes, "don't worry. They are going to die tonight."

CHAPTER 6

Gathering of the Five and a Mind That Got Lost

The plan had been for Jacob and me to meet Hess and some others at a place that we called the pond, a regular meeting spot to party. It was a piece of land owned by Hess' family that was perfect for getting together. I intended to be there even if the validity of my friend's and my sanity was in jeopardy because of that foul mixture in the bottle. I had become increasingly convinced that it couldn't be anything less than evil based on my experience so far. And by the way, Jacob would've surely concurred.

"Maybe," I thought, "Azzore had finally found it necessary to spew his wrath upon me."

It wasn't until we turned off the desolate country road onto the dirt path leading to the pond that the thought took root that maybe Jacob could be coming apart from within. It wasn't just his eyes that raised suspicion, but his stale and vehement stare. It possessed a ghost which looked back at me behind his thick glasses and grinned like some dead animal.

But then I thought, while staring at him as I crept toward the pond along the rock-littered path through the forest, maybe it was I who was losing his shit. How could I accuse my friend of such things when he was merely sitting there? Strangely postured like an arthritic baby perhaps, but still just sitting.

Could I be the mad one? Is that how this vile stuff worked? Had it begun to spin my mind around, waging a war of hemispheres in my head?

These questions haunted me like a mean dead uncle. Hundreds of possible variants teetered around my conscious. At one point, I even spoke aloud and asked myself, "have I lost my sanity?"

Before I could descend any further into a lively pit of madness, the narrow dirt road opened into a vast circular clearing with the treeline bordering the grass. We had arrived at the pond. The scene was picturesque. It resembled a sketch that would accompany a story in some classic folk-tale. It was mystique and elegant. Where the treeline skated around the clearing, the grass spread out away from the forest for several hundred feet all around. Then it dipped gradually as the landscape fell away making an obtuse slant forming a deep bowl where the pond lay at the bottom, resting beneath the opened sky.

I parked at the bottom of the slope near the water's edge. Our friends were already there with their backs to the pond and a full, pale moon reflected on the water behind them, casting a ghostly residue over the water. At first, they were merely diaphanous silhouettes in the darkness, but when I stepped closer, I could see Hess and his girlfriend, Lena. Behind them, sitting on her car was Lena's best friend, Helen.

In a small town, most everyone gets labeled, and Lena and Helen were no exceptions. They were both seen by everyone as being hippies and maybe it was true. They were deemed respectable in some ways, and each was considered to be different in her weird way.

Lena loved the earth and everything on it. She believed wholeheartedly that nature was alive with spirits that existed all around us in everything from the wind and water to the grass and trees. Lena dressed plainly, mostly in simple-kind of dresses and often wore a flower in her hair. She was a lover of folk music and danced with bells on her shoes when the mood was right. She sometimes recited poetry, even when no one cared to hear it.

Helen, on the other hand, possessed more flare and darkness in her persona. Although she was Lena's best friend, she didn't care so much for the earth as she did guys. She was known for being promiscuous and was looked down upon by most people because of it. Ironically, she embraced her bad reputation. She wore dark clothes that matched her straight black hair and off-set her vampiric pale skin. Her strongest quality, I thought, was her love of the art of Salvador Dali. Sometimes I could sense how she would get lost within the nectar of her own words as she deciphered his most intriguing and dazzling paintings, finding meanings in each stroke that I would never have noticed without her.

Once outside in the fresh, more sensible air, I felt a little more at ease again. It was better out here than in the restraint of my car, where sanity seemed stretched thin. The mighty jolt of badness that had wrecked my senses had been replaced by a soothing kind of warmth now. The setting was picturesque as if nature's own masterpiece.

Insects chirped, far-off a fish splashed somewhere in the pond causing the water to ripple against the muddy bank. Wafting through the air, the smoke from the cigarettes glided across the water and traced the thin shadows of the treetops on the reflection of the moon in the silvery water. All of this was a natural sedative for my wrecked senses.

It didn't take long for Hess and the other to know there was something wrong with us. It was my bizarre eyes and lame expression that gave me away. For Jacob, maybe it was that he went directly to the water's edge and knelt. After several minutes of staring at his reflection, he began tapping at it softly, watching his face continuously break away in tiny rivulets.

"You guys already dropped? What the hell, dude? Couldn't you wait?" Hess asked.

"No," I replied sternly, "no I couldn't. You weren't there, man. You didn't see his eyes."

Hess looked at me as if I had murdered someone he loved. "What? What the fuck does that even mean?" He then laughed at my crude state of mind.

Lena, standing beside Hess with her arms around his waist said, "Who cares? Just give us some already."

The part of me was still somewhat reasonable and wanted to keep the nasty poison away from them, but the other part of me controlled by the insidious chemical wanted to share its power. It told me, without speaking, but through caressing my thoughts, that it was too good to ever explain with any clarity to anyone – that they would never believe its power. It was true. Every gear I was slung into was stronger and more intense than anything I had ever experienced.

I had to show them.

The sane part of me hesitated; I still didn't know its full potential or its intent. To unleash something this potent and feral could be disastrous.

But that was just madness talking.

Right?

After having felt the hideous cold caress of the demon fidgeting in my conscious and recognizing its power for what it was, I was especially wary of allowing Helen to take such an overwhelming and sly drug. It was only the year before, in the heat of the summer, that I had witnessed her lose her mind.

One morning, Hess and I were attempting to nurse one bastard of a hangover with marijuana and aspirin, when I received a strange call from a hysterical Lena. She was convinced that Helen had lost her mind and incidentally couldn't find it anywhere. The intensified urgency whipping in Lena's voice suggested that we hurry, for the dilemma was escalating to unimaginable proportions.

Shortly later, we arrived at Lena's house. She was wearing an extra-large Grateful Dead t-shirt that hugged her knees. As she approached, obviously distressed, she informed us that her parents were out of town and that she and Helen had brewed a pot of 'magic coffee' from a batch of mushroom juice Hess and I had concocted for them the day before.

This brew had been especially strong, so much so, that it could've been deemed godly. The shrooms weren't just boiled and jarred; they were carefully managed and expertly extracted. More than fifty fresh caps had been mashed inside a torn pantyhose leg and tied off before placed in about five cups of boiling water. The enclosed shrooms were then mashed and rolled around as they boiled so that the poison could be squeezed precisely from the caps, before being left to simmer for ten minutes. The finished product was nothing short of magical.

We found Helen in the backyard hovering ominously over a small dog named Fifi. Her hair was a frenzied mess, and it sounded as if she was speaking some lazy gibberish that barely left the tip of her tongue.

She held Fifi down forcibly on its back with one hand and had a stick in her other hand prodding it around in its mouth. Obviously coerced by the friendly poison, she devoutly believed she had lost her mind and that Fifi had found it and eaten it.

I kept my distance. My hangover was far too intense for what was happening. Helen's slovenly appearance made her seem like a staggering zombie uprooted from its grave and trying to make friends with a terrified dog.

She seemed to grow more furious by the second and the obstreperous inflection she used as she yelled made her words incomprehensible to me.

"Give it to me you motherfucker!" She growled, "It's mine!"

Lena was trying not to spin out of control herself. But it was half-expected by now, for when something maniacal and unreasonable happens while you're in the midst of a trip, the consequences in your mind are rather unpredictable, but almost certainly very bad.

I tried to imagine what could have brought Helen to that creatively mad point. It makes one wonder just where a person's mind must go to be perceived as lost. And where does one's mind go to believe somehow a tiny dog must regurgitate it? There must have been some psycho-reproductive process that took place to manifest such reversion of self-awareness.

It is quite funny how things turn out sometimes.

Understandably, we all were afraid to touch her. After all, without her mind to discern her actions, who could know just what she was capable of? I could hear Lena drolly shouting, "let him go, Helen! He doesn't have it!"

Hess was trying to coax her into just letting him go, which was odd because the way in which he spoke to her was in the very way you would talk to your dog to convince it to let go of a newspaper, or maybe a shoe.

"Come on, girl. Let him go. You can do it," he was saying as he clapped his hands together.

From where I was standing, at a completely safe and neutral distance, I could see the fear in Fifi's eyes. I could also see the fear crystalizing into desperation. He was starting to snarl and gnash his teeth in a way that warned he was willing to take her fingers if she didn't stop.

Lena and Hess were wasting their breaths trying to utilize any reason with her when there no longer was any. There was no convincing her in any way that was sane in the least bit. To negate the feral logic brooding in our presence and bring control with reason back to the situation it was detrimental that we thought as if we too had lost our minds. I quickly began to imagine the situation as if it were a riddle. All riddles must have an answer, no matter how silly or outlandish they seem.

I asked myself: If someone believes to have lost their mind, how can you help them find it?

I answered myself: One cannot literally lose their mind.

So, how then do you make that person, which is solely convinced, realize that they have not?

One word kept formulating in my head: DISTRACTION.

It was then that a surge of adrenaline helped me quickly devise a genius plan. I found Helen's purse inside and hid it in the mailbox by the road. I then subtly suggested to her that she probably left her mind in her purse and that maybe she should check it to be safe and sure.

"After all, women tend to keep everything in their purses," I told her.

This possibility seemed appropriate, and she immediately let go of the dog. It flipped over onto its feet and scurried to Lena's outstretched arms with a look of terror straining its eyes. Helen then spent the next two hours looking for her purse. By the time she finally found it in the mailbox, she had forgotten all about losing her mind.

Hess had already started a small fire in a hole he had dug out in the dirt. It breathed warmth and light on us as we stood in the grass. I held the bottle up to the glow and teased everyone with the darkness inside of it. Gazing upon it, I felt that same foreboding sense I felt at Chris' house. It scared me still, and I couldn't pacify the feeling that its hooks were in me and that I was the puppet.

Hess took the bottle from me and dropped it on each of their tongues. There was no hesitation from any of them or any hint that I could glean to suggest that any of them felt the same force from the bottle permeating our space.

I wanted to stop them. The urge to do something dramatic, like slap their faces before the venom reached their tongues, nearly crippled me. I was in no shape to babysit four bad trips – or even one! – especially out in the wild amongst other beasts.

None of what I thought or felt mattered anymore. Whatever would happen, would happen, because now we had all partook and the sacrifice was almost complete. We were all destined for either a blessing or a curse. You never can tell until it's too late.

The soothing rhythms of Sublime mingled with the slight breeze and blessed my ears. We were all smoking and talking as they waited for the acid to tip them over the edge. That is all of us except Jacob, who was still at the pond tracing his face with the tips of his fingers in the water. I thought of asking him to join, but it was his trip and who was I to ruin it?

As I lit a Kool and felt the nice menthol burn in my throat, Hess asked me to tell the girls of The Trip. I didn't want to. I wanted to be left to my own boundless imagination, but after some pressuring I conceded. I managed to piece together enough sense to make my sentences intelligible and clear to tell the story as they gathered in silence in the firelight.

CHAPTER 7

The Prophetic Trip

It was 1999 and my friend Daniel and I had decided to eat mescaline for the first time. I had just graduated high school, and he had joined the army, so what better way to celebrate our paths but by delving into the unknown.

There was a party being thrown by a rich girl named Kala at her phenomenally structured home. She was a pharmaceutical representative and had just landed a job in Texas. This was to be her going away party, which just so happened to be the last night before Daniel went to boot camp; so it was almost as if it was pre-determined for this to be our first ride.

We got there just in time. The mescaline had taken its time to work, but just as we arrived at the party, it began creeping up my spine like a monstrous midget. That's when I knew that I should hold on tight.

The first problem I encountered was parking, because, of course, there was nowhere for it. A narrow dead-end street in a wealthy neighborhood and a small grass lawn isn't exactly the ideal place for sixteen cars to park, especially those of us caught in the sharp claws of mescaline.

I remember Daniel saying with sound and stunning conviction, "Just fucking park in the back."

"Of course," I thought. "How logical and simple." I jumped the curb and as gracefully as a man snagged in the grip of a powerful hallucinogen could manage, I cut through the neighbor's yard. It was a prestigious example of a well-kept lawn with perfectly mowed grass and a fabulous array of flowers marching up the brick walkway that led to a colossal house which had more windows that I had ever seen. There was a sign posted that read ‘no fishing' in the grass, which I noticed just before I smashed it with my truck.

The words confused my intelligence for a moment and seared within my memory. At the time, for only a moment, I couldn't understand its meaning or its purpose for being there. I drove like a coked-out drag racer not seeing the goldfish pond in front of me. I drove over and through it bumping my head on the roof as my tires tore across it violently, splashing a glorious wave that showered the hood and windshield of my car. For one unclear moment, I even thought that I saw one of the goldfish flying past my window with a frozen, terrified look masking its face. Unsure of what else to do, I quickly swerved, carving a zig-zagging shallow trench across the grass.

I came to a stop in Kala's backyard, finally, and remember incredible loud music shaking the windows of my car. The harsh and ravage sounds of White Zombie were murdering everything around me, and I loved it. Over the music, I could vaguely hear Daniel laughing uncontrollably at what I had done. I suppose, under the circumstances, it was quite funny, so I joined him in sharing a maniacal fit of hilarity. This lasted a while, tickle-fits are unavoidable while tripping.

The second problem that I faced was Kala. She had been waiting for me to get out of the truck while Daniel and I were dying in laughter. Over the roar of the blasting music, she hit my windows like an angry vagrant. I didn't care. I was in the moment, and the moment reigned under hilarity, not aggression.

Once we could laugh no more, we got out of the car, and instantly Kala came at me like a miffed bee, buzzing strange words in heated anger. It took my mind a bit to catch up with what was happening. The spontaneous change in environment – from a jovial experience to a peeved girl shaking her fists at me – tweaked my senses in an odd way. I was seriously confused, unaware now of what appalling space I had bumped into.

She was short and had the biggest breasts I had ever seen, but my attention was focused on her furrowed eyebrows conveying to me that she was abnormally furious. The way that she huffed and puffed, stomping her feet emphatically as she trotted towards me, reminded me of a caricature of some hairy brute in a classic cartoon, chasing a little guy with his chest flexed as he mouthed intimidating words.

"What the fuck are you doing? You just tore up my neighbor's yard and killed her fucking fish! You fucking asshole!"

She was rather livid, more so than expected by me, and to be completely honest her attitude and behavior gave me a raw vibe that I knew would be hard to shake. The time had come for change. This environment was oppressive and seemed to me to be unhealthy to my trip. I felt that I had to take control of the moment and turn it around in my favor; for the sake of my sanity.

"What the fuck do you mean?" I staidly asked, yet with an accusatorily firm accent. I gave her a moment to contemplate my meaning and noticed that her brows lowered. Her face loosened as she stared at me. It was then that I asked, "You don't want me to park back here?"

She continued to stare at me as if I were the anti-Christ. She was befuddled by my matter-of-fact tone and seemed to withdraw some anger.

"What the hell do you mean? You destroyed my neighbor's yard. What the fuck am I gonna tell them?"

She pointed at the yard while raising her voice again. I could see the sign laying broken in a rutted yard. I saw the watery grave that was once a goldfish pond, now ruined. I saw the damage, and I sensed her concern. I just didn't care. The moment desperately had to be controlled and reversed. This anger didn't jive well with my trip which was now beginning to tighten around my mind like a boa constrictor.

"They are going to be so pissed," she continued. Now, she seemed to be talking to herself.

"Perhaps," I thought, "her mind had broken somehow, and she was going on some kind of reserve switch in her conscious that allowed her to speak bewilderedly to herself to keep from internally combusting." I felt now that it was time to leave her, but I knew that I must say something to end the terrible moment. I could see now that changing it wasn't an option anymore. It had to be killed. Just walking away as she spoke would be inappropriate with all things put into consideration.

I plotted my dialogue carefully. The mescaline assaulted my thoughts, and everything else within that makes me, which was now making this situation extremely difficult.

"Don't tell them anything," I said sternly, "and if you do, I'll come to find you. Do you understand? I'll fucking come for you."

She said nothing. Perhaps it was my authoritative, father-like tone. I knew not to apologize because I had thought to apologize, and the mind is a terrible thing to trust while being raped by such a drug as mescaline.

So then, I thought, what was I doing? How could I know if anything I was doing was sane?

The important thing to understand while tripping really hard is that thinking gets you into situations such as this one and that there comes the point during your journey (good or bad) to just stop thinking and learn to go with your body instead. So, I walked away. The timing was right because the moment of silence had lingered long enough. Her mouth was opened in perhaps a fearful expression as I left her there with the silence to comfort her.

As I walked away, I saw Daniel from the corner of my eye, which was good because I had forgotten him. My mind had been too busy plotting against me with cowardly plans to ravage my way of thinking. I wondered, though, if he was in any way as mentally demented as I was.

Out of nowhere, I felt as if my stride was slanted, or maybe the ground was spinning slowly vertically in a spiraled formation that was impossible to see but could be felt. I slowed my pace, considerably, and minded my surroundings, paying closer attention to the things not usually noticed, because these were the fuckers to look out for.

Under the pallid moonlight, there was a Praying Mantis shadow boxing soulfully in blades of grass glowing with a gentle green hue. His jabs were crisp, and hooks were even quicker.

"Jesus! Would you look at the reach on that bastard? He's like Thomas Hearns, dammit!" I said to no one in particular as I turned to Daniel to show him the tiny fighter.

It was then I found my third problem, Daniel. A transformation had occurred, and I had seen it before. His face was drawn tight because of a crude and leering grin. His eyes, which should've been eclipsed by his huge pupils, were hidden by his swollen eyelids. He had gone completely deranged in only a matter of a few minutes.

I should have expected this. When it came to mushrooms and LSD, he was apt to commit devious actions and display borderline psychotic behavior. So then why should I ever have expected mescaline to be any different?

Although it had never been medically proven, it was believed by many to be some sort of chemical imbalance inside him. I, for one, attributed it to a more simple and primal way of reason – the wandering and lonesome god of the nether world, Azzore.

Yes, I should've known that he would reach this grinding gear inevitably. But perhaps I knew and just didn't care subconsciously, being that he was great entertainment while losing his mind. Besides, he was leaving to serve his country the next day, so why the hell not experiment with dementia the last night of freedom?

For the moment, my thoughts were detuned from Daniel and his potential meltdown hastily approaching by the sound of horridly bad music that only rich kids listen to and the smell of cigarette smoke infused with alcohol coming from around the corner of the house in the front yard. I peeked at the scene and saw cars parked in the grass and in the street. At least thirty people littered the yard talking in scattered groups. I shambled across the yard and motioned for Daniel to follow; his face was still carved by an exaggerated grin that made him look like a devil. I had to keep an eye on him, I thought, God forbid he started screaming like an upset toddler and began chasing innocent people into the street.

The mescaline was charging through me like a Mongolian army raiding a village. I could taste my teeth in the back of my throat. The night sky had become a playground for me and the stars. They danced and played, making shapes for me to guess. I had stopped walking and had begun to stare at the heavens above the crowd of people.

Suddenly, I felt that something was wrong. I had been oblivious to the fact that while I had been distracted by the sprightful stars, the aura of the entire atmosphere around me had changed. I felt eyes scolding me.

But why?

I looked down and saw Daniel lying on his back in the grass. He was mumbling esoterically, but I understood him to say something about a warm pool as he waved his arms gracefully through the blades of grass.

Yes, I should have known not to feed him mescaline.

"What the hell are you up to, man? Are you trying to embarrass me? Get up, you crazy bastard!" I shouted accidentally.

He had the serene look of an old man fishing silently in solitude – which was scary to me in a way. He spoke only one word that I could understand: swimming.

"You have to get up, man! I can't protect you from these hideous bastards. There's . . . ." I couldn't finish what I wanted to say because of a pulverizing sense of dread. It sat on me like a fat grandmother. My eyes floated away from my friend swimming in the grass onto a sizeable crowd of people I couldn't recognize. They all were staring at me and not the mindless madman at my feet mumbling incoherent words.

There was only one sensible and responsible thing to say at a moment like this. "Don't worry everyone; he's just tripping. He's not really swimming. It's under control, really."

Sadly, this explanation didn't suffice. Alluring paranoia crept in and clawed deep within my stomach. They were still watching me, some I believe even booed me as if I had just given a bad performance. I had to leave. There was no other solution. The mission had failed and the moment here at this place had gone to a fervid, stinking hell. Their eyes were burning my skin. I knew that they would never let us leave alive. They would tear us apart like crazed piranhas. I knew this without even knowing somehow. It was a strong feeling I had deep inside that I just couldn't ignore. These were the bastards that I knew would come for me howling for blood. I had already killed the goldfish, and now my friend thought he was a fish. These bastards couldn't understand; nor could ever condone such behavior.

There was only one option.

I calmly lit a cigarette and stepped over Daniel. I, rather drolly, walked out of the yard and into the street. I could not be Daniel's lifeguard. I had to leave him; this I knew, undoubtedly. I had to be alone. The mescaline was gnawing at my mind with serrated teeth like some junkie rat. The dull crowd of people judging me and the shitty music they played while doing it put me on the verge of lashing out in a dark homicidal manner only a detested fiend would understand. I could feel something coming; something happening soon, and I could only hope that Daniel would be okay alone.

.....

I walked along the desolate street tinkering with what thoughts dripped from my drowning mind. It felt as if I were walking backward, or in a dream, perhaps even walking backward in a dream. I was in an unfamiliar place, and all the street lights seemed too bright. I squinted and swayed as I walked like a dizzy hobo.

From somewhere beyond the strength of the street lights, in an abysmal darkness beyond me came a screeching kind of bark. I discerned it to be a small dog, or either a large bat, with the clarity I had left still dangling from my logic. I gazed into the dark near the direction the sound had emerged from, waiting for something to happen. Another bark pierced through the black veil of night. I stepped towards the sound and stopped again when I noticed something looming like a giant in the dull hint of light away from the street. It was a stunning white house with an immaculate yard. Not knowing what I should do next I just stood there.

I heard the bark again, followed by a child-like voice. It tenderly said to me, "come and play with me."

Instead of questioning my sanity I followed the phantom voice. In all realms of impossibilities, the idea that it came from an actual child reigned supreme. For I knew it had to have come from the dog.

I stepped onto the soft grass and felt the cool grass jumble between my toes.

What the piss, I thought? Where were my shoes? I surely didn't recall removing them.

I paced myself, for my balance was off, and walked around the side of the house to the backyard. Some primeval part of me knew that a dog exasperating a child's innocent voice and formulating actual words was improbable. But was it at all possible? I asked myself. Because I had heard it clearly. It appeared at this point that all logic had surely been decimated and that was fine with me. It was better this way.

Only the moonlight lit the backyard. The dog was nowhere in sight, and I thought this to be a rude welcoming. I called to it, but it never came. Had it called me here to watch me in some covert position and laugh as I stood there looking stupid?

I was barefoot, alone, confused, and mentally challenged by the mighty drug warping my perception. The moon painted the lawn that spread out below me a pallid tint comparable to the dry ashes of the dead. I stood there, being washed by the moonlight, completely unaware of anything. Again, I found myself watching the stars. Under their glory, and the moon's shower of light, I could feel myself evolving. Time and presence played no part in anything, nor would they ever any longer. The strangest part of all of this is that it wasn't as painful as one might expect. The idea of hyper-evolution seems scary and out-right hell on the body – both externally and internally – but there in the stranger's yard, it was quite elative. I had somehow, without being aware, found the shadow of myself cast by a baleful moon.

The blades of grass became soft and gel-like, then suddenly it felt as if I were in a warm bath. Without warning, my soul wailed and wanted to take a swim. I laid down, sinking into the melting cushion of grass. As I lay there, separated from reality in ecstasy within the unknown, I realized that Daniel hadn't been mad after all. I then felt sorry for leaving him alone with the pack of rude animals that didn't understand the journey we had to take.

I opened my eyes and saw the sky spread out above me like an electric canopy with the stars glistening and moving about like bees in a black meadow. My mind was dizzy, and my eyes found it difficult to keep up with the constant pushing and pulling of the bedazzled night sky. I couldn't look away, though, their dance was for too enchanting to even dare such a sin.

All at once, like a scene of war, the stars began to fire back and forth at one another, exploding in blossoms of shimmery colors upon impact. The red mist of stardust left in the wake sifted in the moonlight through space's deepest region and slowly began to take a mysterious form. Minutes later I was gazing upon a red face, gazing down upon me from the eastern sky. The features of it were like that of a god's. Its eyes harbored every soul alive it seemed. I knew, somehow, that I was staring at the face of Jesus.

His head bowed, and his eyes sparkled alive, the stardust which had formed Him danced in reddish waves causing His hair to sway as he glowered at me. I remember feeling as though saying something was appropriate, but what do you say to the face of Jesus baring down on you as you're struck out on mescaline?

"Please don't eat me," I said with quivering lips. This seemed perfectly logical because His teeth were utterly gigantic.

Finding my question funny, He cocked His head back into the black space behind Him and bellowed boisterous laughter that shook the remaining stars from the sky. They fell in silvery showers across the earth like broken spider-webs.

From behind the ardent face, at an angle from the northeast sky, I saw a conflagrant streak slashing through the darkness, leaving a charred scar lingering in its wake as it sped at me, raging closer behind the face in the sky. I felt that I should've shouted something like, "Jesus, look out man!" But the words froze in my throat before reaching my tongue. The great ball of light inched closer to Him, its tail burning with fire behind it. The closer it got His face, the brighter it became as its reddish glow bled through the heavens.

It was here where things finally began to get weird. The monolithic face's mouth opened slowly and silently mouthed the words, 'oh shit,' just before the burning ball of light blasted a hole through the back of its head and out of the front between the eyes. His entire face shattered into billions of pieces like a mirror in the sky, but somehow miraculously conflated with the speeding cannon of light descending to destroy me – so it seemed.

I know that no rational human being would ever find themselves in this strange moment. Obviously, the moment that the reddened face of Jesus tried to eat them they would have found someplace to hide, considering they were even mad enough to find themselves that unlucky.

But I have never proclaimed myself rational or sane, that I can remember anyway, so I stood to my feet and watched the final seconds as it descended towards me. Its arch was massive, a crescentic streak slicing the pitch-black sky. I could hear wheezing as it got closer, sounding like a banshee dying as it gives birth. The nearer that it got, the clearer it was for me to observe that the burning ball was indeed more of a head with a tortured face plummeting to the earth, presumably right at my feet. Its eyes were closed, pinched shut, perhaps from the intense heat and velocity by which it moved. It seemed to wince as if in unnatural pain revealing gritted teeth that danced around in its mouth like flames.

I couldn't move; I could only stand, but I couldn't see. I could only stare.

In one great blast before me, it struck the earth, and my entire body shook with the ground. Almost instantly, the earth below me spewed from itself a radiant spectrum of unrecognizable colors like some cosmic geyser. I could feel the importance of its power and thought to myself that this can't be real.

Could it?

Normally I could depend on reason and sharp senses to decipher such anomalies, but when your reality as you perceive it to be constructs vivid figments born from imagination, this is impossible.

In other words, when your idea of reality shits a giant deity from the heavens at your feet, you're pretty much fucked out of your ability to rationalize anything with reason. This was as real as life at that moment.

The earth vomited an array of otherworldly colors back up into the outer reaches of the heavens as I stared only feet away, unable to flinch a muscle. Shadows from the colors, which I never knew before but were real enough to taste and feel, peeled from the eruption and spread evenly in the air forming puffs of beauty that resembled clouds. It occurred to me in that sublime moment that I was witnessing a strong orgasm by our Earth, brought on by the descending face.

The volcano of transcendence erupting from the depths of earth faded after some time. The ambient clouds that had formed overhead had begun to swell so much that they were drizzling the molten remnants of the alien colors in both skinny and obese streaks down from above me. After the clouds were drained and were empty, they were sucked away into a hungry void in the sky. I began to taste the immortal-like colors less and feel their phosphorous odor leaving my senses as the vortex left. There was only the comfort of darkness, and I was finally able to glean my surrounding. I was still barefoot. The grass still felt warm between my toes. The air was still cool and clean. The stranger's yard seemed to be like my fertile mind, being that it could become whatever I desired.

In front of me, where the orgasmic eruption exploded from the split in the earth, sat some sort of wondrously large yellow frog. It was about the size of a small dog and squatted in the grass facing me from exactly the point of origin of the volcano. It stared at me with lazy, puppy-like eyes and yawned like a groggy stripper after a long night.

What the hell was it? Some sort of cosmic organism? Some amphibious progeny from the face in the sky?

Or was this just a figment of my warped perception?

Of course, all of these seemed like perfectly plausible explanations, because perhaps a warped perception is all we've ever really had. So, what is actuality and what is not?

My mind was tumbling in reverse.

Whatever this strange alien was, it began to slide across the lawn like a snail on a flat piece of glass. I expected for it to hop, walk on its hands, or speak to me in sign language – anything but creepily slither the way that it did. It slid across my feet and its smooth, yet leathery, underside felt cold and damp. The feeling made me shiver. It moved slowly, pushing itself on its belly like a condom filled with jelly. Its slimy texture glowed like a cat's eyes hiding in the night. Trailing behind it, expelling from its body as it slid, was a ghostly yellow apparition that vaporized into the air and hovered stagnantly a couple of feet off the ground.

I didn't have to ask, nor did I. I just knew by some predisposed engraining within myself that I was to follow the yellow mist.

I crawled listlessly, following the glowing trail and minding the progeny in front of me; everything except for it was untouched blackness in the dizzying sea of darkness. Only the slithering creature and the mist served as my light as it slugged onward like a drunk man on slick ice.

After a few moments, the amphibious-like creature stopped ahead of me. Like an owl, its head spun completely around without moving its body and gazed at me with its sad, lazy eyes. I stopped and marveled at the unique specimen that I couldn't understand. It blinked slowly with its tongue hanging out of its mouth and in a cracking high-pitched tone, like a ventriloquist talking for his dummy, said, "take my hand." It held its hand out, extending three elongated, crooked fingers pointing at me to grab. I took them and felt them wrap around my knuckles with a wet, cold grip.

What was happening here? Had I really reached the deranged point to where I was holding hands with strange life forms?

More importantly, what was God thinking sending me this creature?

Suddenly, with my limp hand in its grasp, the creature began to deflate rapidly and fly wildly through the air, carrying me with it. The sound was like a large balloon losing air as it whizzed me higher, carrying me higher like a kite in a wind-storm brushing from right to left and top to bottom, even in full and half circles. I remember being within reach of the highest point of some tree and its naked branches scratching at my face just before I began to fall. The creature had crumbled into the cool air, and I was falling helplessly, unable to save myself even with my mad imagination. I began to scream but the wind battering my face as I fell choked my cries, filling my throat as I tasted the night air.

It was here that my shadow, I believe, separated from my conscious body and invited me to pass through, unbound, and faithfully search for enlightenment.

I stopped falling. I stopped trying to scream and found myself blinded by an abundance of light that was drowning out everything. I could feel it crawling on my skin, then had to close my eyes to stop the penetrating contrast. When I opened them, I found that I was sitting in a wide room with walls made from bamboo, tied tightly with a tough twine, and was decorated with foreign art forms of children riding hairy mythological beasts with big eyes and blunt teeth. Words were scrolled on papyrus hung loosely from the stick walls; they were of some ancient symbolism that I couldn't decipher.

As I perused the room longer, I began to see that the solar system began to appear in a thin mist all around me. After merely seconds the mist had dissolved and celestial bodies lay scattered like snowflakes stuck in the air. Separated from the misty planets, the sun shone like a great serpent's head in the wall in front of me, and the moon drank from its power behind me. The planets swam in disarray around me as if floating in some chaotic sea.

Hanging by thin, hardly noticeable, strings falling from a black abyss was a large yellow and scaly dragon. It swayed side to side and back and forth slowly as if trapped under water. Though it seemed to be a mere puppet bound by the strings its mouth opened and closed slowly like a dying fish. Its eyes were frozen in a blank dead stare that still somehow stayed upon me as it swayed.

I remember feeling sick. All of the screaming light and objects moving in dream-like motion was taking a toll on my mind. No man should ever have to endure such a trip unless that man is properly prepared. I felt the desirable urge to leave, but there was no door or any passage for me to take. I thought of diving into the sun ahead of me only I couldn't move. I was stuck where I knelt, held hostage by my own doing.

The bastards surely had me now.

There was nothing subtle happening here. My mind had become sick with dizziness, and there was no escape. I had climbed into the warm womb of madness - and the fucked-up part is that I was beginning to feel comfortable there.

Did this make me mad?

The wall began to fade to black in front of me. The moon was starting to lose its glow without the energy of the sun to sustain it. Still, its luminous arms of light reached out and over me sinking into everything around me combating the impending darkness. With the air-breathing dimness, I heard heavy and rough breaths, so loud and deep that my heart shrank from the intrusive noise. In the center of this dreamscape, between all the heavenly bodies, the yellow dragon began to growl and shake with great tremors. It huffed like roaring thunder from within its loins and opened its mouth wider to reveal a colony of sharp teeth. Its eyes were no longer dead-like and still, but instead, were alive with hunger.

Right before me, the bastard was coming to life. The strings had broken now, and only its wings kept it afloat. I was muddled and stricken dumb with fear. I mean, Jesus, I was in reach of the evil bastard.

Its eyes began to burn with a deep green ember as they stalked me. I continued to shiver and convulse as it huffed and moaned deep within its hellish stomach. Its mouth opened and I saw its teeth again. They were like the jutted peaks of mountains aligned in a puzzling formation of several rows, some even overlapping others. Blue smoke escaped from its belly through its mouth and nostrils then quickly filled the room. I panted from fear and confusion as the blue mist from the dragon's body entered my lungs. My eyes burned incessantly; all I could do was close them to cease the blue burn and ebb the churning fire in my soul.

In the darkness that I had created for my own piece of mind, I could hear the beastly growls and hisses. I could feel the smoke enveloping me still and smell its acrid odor. I sensed the heat from its serpent-like body as it inched closer in this unfamiliar place. I was truly, mortally, afraid and could think of only one thing to say aloud. With my eyes closed and my heart drumming, I whispered, "please don't eat me."

The words came naturally enough, for I truly didn't want to be eaten alive. The very thought of being chewed while helpless and dissolved with the saliva of some big goddamned serpent with wings mortified me. Even more crude and indecent is the thought that after being broken down and digested by the vile acid in its stomach, I'd become dragon shit, and that's not a destiny anyone would want.

Luckily just as soon as I had spoken to it, the sounds began to descend into the vast nothing I had stumbled upon. The heat from its breath and body faded. I forced the courage to open my eyes and found that the sun had returned and shone loudly in front of me on the bamboo wall. The planets to my right were at peace now, swaying somewhat in order. Most importantly, the dragon was still again. It hung from the invisible ceiling as if under the control of some supreme puppeteer.

But there was a difference now.

Beneath the yellow dragon, suspended recumbently from the abyss above, was a large rectangular table with short legs that made it almost kiss the floor of light. It was garnished perfectly with a red tablecloth of fine silk. It had some foreign symbolism sewn ruggedly to it. I don't know how I knew, but somehow, I knew the ancient language read, 'damnation.'

In the center of the table was a large silver pitcher with a golden handle. Manifesting from the strange air, four silver cups appeared at each corner of the table. I could hear a vibrant rumble of wind approaching from somewhere that couldn't be tracked.

Then the smell of perfume intoxicated my nerves.

I never saw her appear, but in front of me at the table was a silhouette of a woman robed in white, moving flawlessly in a circle around the table. She floated like an angel playing in the clouds, her feet hidden underneath the glorious white robe hovering inches from the ground. Her hypnotizing silhouette seemed to swim in the rebirth of light. She was indeed a phantom of the purest beauty, and my eyes were delighted to drink her in.

As I watched her sift magically around the table, her features became clearer. Her hair was black and fixed in a tight bun that peeked above her from the back. It was held together by two red sticks crossing each other as they stuck out over the top. Her face was pleasantly rounded and painted white, but her eyes were painted blue which streaked out above her rose-red cheekbones. She wore a Komodo with the same kind of mysterious hieroglyph embroidered on it in gold, only now I couldn't understand the meaning like I could before.

Then she stopped. She eloquently paused at the center of the table facing me, but not seeing me. She was at the pitcher and reached for it with ghostly pale hands. From the twisted bun in her hair, she removed some sort of sharp stone resembling a diamond, only more enticing. Holding her free hand over the silver gold-handled pitcher, she cut her wrist with the diamond and let her blood fill it until a single streak swam down the side and soaked into the table cloth. She lifted her wrist to her mouth and licked the gaping gash. As her tongue massaged the wound, it healed before my eyes. Leaving the cutting-stone on the table, she took the pitcher and drifted around the table filling each of the silver cups.

Something was happening here. Something that I couldn't understand. I felt that there was something else ready to happen. Her presence had caused a seismic-like shift in my inner-self. I felt no fear as if I was finally safe and didn't feel disoriented, although I certainly was. The great dragon that had wanted to devour me still hovered over her and the table idly watching as she filled the last cup, but somehow, she controlled it; this I could sense. I felt that it feared her.

Incidentally, I began to fear the fact that I didn't fear her. Should I be at peace internally in the presence of some unknown being that held that kind of power?

I tried to swallow the tangible panic rising like heat within me.

After pouring from the pitcher, she put it in the center of the table then turned and bowed to the sun. As she did this, all the celestial bodies by my side suddenly ceased. Everything was frozen in its place. Again, I'm not sure how I knew, but I knew, that time itself had stood still in this moment.

As the woman still bowed to it, the sun began to fade like a tarnished painting. Its fiery glow quickly became a desolate and dark speck among us. Darkness swelled and shrouded me. The pale light from the moon began to fade again behind me as the sun became a frozen rock and vanished into a silent disintegration. It began to get cold as the glow from the planets and from the mysterious woman became the only light present. I saw ice form before me and cover everything around me like a blanket. The dragon began to crystallize as it too froze mercilessly. First, its head broke from its body and crashed to the ground in hundreds of pieces of frozen chunks of blood and flesh. The wings fell next, followed by the rest until it lay in thousands of pieces on the table and floor. The chunks of its carcass sparkled in the restricted amount of light glowing the room.

The planets, too, had become ice. A steamy mist escaped from their shells in the faint pallor of the room. They hung in the black void to my right, suspended by whatever power the woman possessed.

The white-robed woman glowed like a ghost in the darkness. Panging fear stoned my insides once again. The comfort that had just been with me had vanished along with the warmth and light from the place. The cold was upsetting my bones, and I feared they would snap under the least bit of movement, so I tried my best not to move. She took the first cup in her hands as her pulsating glow gleamed in the silver form and held it to her nostrils, breathing in the scent. She then drank from it while her eyes burned ardently as it flowed down her throat. When she had had her fill, she lowered it slowly from her red-stained lips, and her eyes descended to gray. She turned facing the left wall where the inscribed papyrus flailed and threw the cup at it with majestically slow speed. The blood exploded into a sea of sanguine light that temporarily blinded me. My eyes adjusted and I saw the wall had opened and some kind of cosmic portal had formed with holographic-like tunnels swirling tumultuously. I could hear crying and screaming from some unknown world that was unseen and oblivious to us. Upon closer inspection, I could see tortured faces and bloodied bodies pressed against the outer layer of the transparent tunnels.

My eyes went to the foreign symbol on the tablecloth: DAMNATION.

The female apparition then drank from the second cup, turning to the right side of the place where the planets hung idly in their frozen states. She threw the cup, and again the blood splashed in thick pools of red, painting a new universe as the planets were reborn and redesigned in a new perspective. I saw what were stars but had now melted in space and were a chaotic mixture with the blood oozing a peculiar world. Each new planet was bobbing in a bloody ocean of chaotic puss-like corks lost in a tidal wave.

I watched as the apparition stared at the horrifically beautiful creation. I could hear the tortured cries begging for help to my left and see planets being ravaged by massive waves of blood and star-gore. I thought, just what in Hitler's sore asshole is going on here? It was all too real. How could it be anything but real? It was too improbable to be fake.

Had God been overthrown by this foreign deity and was she now reconstructing time and space in her own perception?

And what kind of sick bitch would just drink her own blood like that?

I could not allow myself to be distracted by such frivolous thoughts. It was imperative that I focused on what was happening because by the looks of everything playing out I could be the only person left intact to record it later.

But who could ever believe such nonsense?

It was as I pondered these dubious questions that the room began to swivel un-orthodoxically backward and then forwards; slowly at first but gradually accelerating. I could see the planets furiously fighting the waves in the bloody sea. I began to feel my mind doing the same as everything around me became submerged in the watery chaos. A dark, murky, red, and thick liquid soaked into everything – even myself. My hair was clumpy and drenched with a deathly stench from the blood of the new god.

Afraid, I thought to myself. Could this be? Am I somehow seeing what it is happening to the world I know from some infinite realm, yet still experiencing the same effects I would if I was there in that time?

It certainly seemed to be the case.

I watched again from the place I sat as it rained blood and the phantom drank from the third cup. She then held the cup away from her body and bowed her head over the table, letting a dense string of blood and saliva drool from her mouth soaking into frozen chunks of dragon pieces. In the black puddle of spit and blood, a form began to take shape of a reptilian-like fetus. It began to grow slowly, writhing in the congealing puddle. I could hear it beginning to shriek as its lungs were filled with the god's life force. The more it choked, the bolder its growl became. I recognized it as being the great yellow dragon. It had been reborn. Its scaly skin was lathered in the vile stew that it wailed in. The mysterious woman stood over the bastard beast, hovering in silence among the upset of balance in the environment we shared, holding the silver cup still and watching the new progeny mature in the putrefying amniotic fluid.

Who I had once believed to be my protector and comforter, now seemed to be birthing the feral demon in some witchy way I didn't understand and feared greatly.

In the dreary glow from the stale reflection of the foaming sea of blood, I could see the female apparition change drastically. Her glorious white robe became tattered and torn; appearing dingy and out-worn. Her skin began to peel as if severely blistered and boils festered in groups on her decaying arms and face. The spiritual phenom blessing my eyes had become a wretched crone.

She threw the third cup that she held at the wall that was directly in front of me across from the table where the sun had been. The blood poured down in a red waterfall crashing onto the frozen slate that was the floor and began to fill the space around me. The place that was now my own prison was drowning as the wall opened into a peerless black emptiness, gushing blood as from the mouth of a dying titan.

Again, my head became sick with distraught fatigue. I wanted nothing more than to end the nightmare. There was some sort of higher power in the form of a demoness changing the concept of time and space, a cosmic portal leading to millions of tortured imprisoned souls to my left, and a screaming goddamn dragon baby growing in a stew of filth in front of me. I began to question my sanity once again. This time, even more sure than before that I had misplaced it.

With no warning, the black void that had been the wall in front of me began to change. Like paint spilling on an empty canvas, the blood from the cup snaked down and spread out over the black hole completely. After it had saturated it there was a single, immaculate portrait left like a piece of art hanging in a museum. It was a painting, indeed, of the entire scene I was a part of and seeing right then and up to the very second that I was seeing it. I could see the decayed, peeling woman casting her spells on the universe, the planets drowning, the beast blossoming in the vile puddle. Undoubtedly, the more curious image depicted was me staring in horror and confusion nearly chest deep in the blood filling the room.

The witch-spirit stared at the picture for a moment and then with astounding fervor turned to face me with furious eyes. Her face was contorted in anger and contempt as she glowered at me in a manner that suggested she never knew of my presence until the blood manifested me in the painting. There was a fire in her eyes. The embers from deep within caused her to glow as if it were a candle behind a thin veil of skin. She opened her mouth and bellowed an unnerving shrill from her belly. Spilling from her mouth as she screamed I saw my entire past spew forth in the form of something like a dream in only a fraction of a second.

She pointed at me with a bony, curled finger and I became stiff with fear, but still unable to move. The beast between us was standing now at full size just as before, its gnarling smile taunting me, and it was screaming wildly as if it were hurt, or hungry. The collaboration between the demoness and the dragon as they wailed unnaturally seemed to draw out my soul from my body and wring it like a used rag.

She grabbed the fourth cup and drank from it as my life spewed forth in a series of demonical chants and screams directed at me. The blood spilled from her cracked and crusted lips. The abhorring clamor deafened me and hurt, but I couldn't begin to move, still. She had some hellish curse on me, and I was bound to the pool of blood.

She then raised the silver cup and hurled it at me. But as it came at me, it hardly moved as if it were moving against a strong continuous wind. Time and space had been altered, so what was, was not and what was not, was what was. So, it seemed.

I still couldn't move. I could only watch as the cup gently came at me in the chaos surrounding me; the blood inside sloshing about in the openness it traveled. In the background, just as the cup crashed into me and covered me in her poisonous blood, I saw the dragon swoop upon her and eat her with one violent bite.

As soon as it was done, I awoke, lying in the grass of the stranger's yard looking up at the stars.

CHAPTER 8

The Trip Continues

I walked back to Kala's house not knowing quite how long I had been away. I couldn't remember getting to where I was. I wasn't even sure that I was where I was at that point.

Was I still in some psychedelic, psychotic meltdown? Or was I trapped in a cubicle of conscious deceit?

The vision I was given had cracked the sky of my reason, and I felt as if I wanted to cry. Although it felt so real, it just couldn't have been.

Could it?

I caught myself in every moment expecting the great yellow dragon to pounce upon me from the darkness and carry my chewed carcass away in its mouth to the center of the moon. No doubt, I had certainly been affected by this vision and wanted desperately to find out what it meant. It still lingered like someone's bad breath in the misty recesses of my conscious.

I made it back to Kala's but didn't know what to make of what I found. Everything was wrong here and immediately made no sense to me. The house was dark inside, not even a porch light burned, and every car was gone.

Everything had vanished.

Gnawing aggravation gripped me, for this was all that I needed; I had just witnessed the end of the world, its rebirth through the shadow of blood and magic, now as the mescaline shifted gears people and cars were vanishing. I began to call out for Daniel, but he didn't answer. I walked around in a stupor examining the scene and calling out Kala's name, or to anyone that may hear. There was no one there; not a single soul stirred but my own. Something was indeed badly wrong. I felt lost just like Alice did after chasing the white rabbit into the hole. I began to wonder if the glowing frog had carried me up through some balance of times and into another dimension of reality and left me stranded. That would certainly explain the desolation.

Or, had the witch goddess sent me here when she doused me with her blood?

Had it all been real? Is that why I was alone?

There had to be a better explanation than that of *Alice In Wonderland.* My mind reeled the possibilities. There were too many questions to be sure of anything. Plus, the mescaline was still crashing through me like a tsunami wave, and the crest was far from breaking. I didn't know how long I had been subdued in the stranger's yard. It could've been hours for all I knew. Everyone could have just simply left. That was, after all, the most plausible and logical scenario.

Only logic and anything plausible had long ago vanished this night. Besides, where was Daniel? He had been with me earlier, this much I was sure of. So, where did that leave me assembling logic to plausibility? Absolutely nowhere. I may as well have been back in the dark goddess's domain of blood.

I wandered around to the backyard and found that my truck was still there. Of course it would be; any attachment to myself would remain mine and with me in another realm of space and time, right? I had hoped to find Daniel sitting inside, confined to only the potion twirling his mind with its power. But there was no one inside.

I was, indeed, alone.

I left the way that I came, through the goldfish pond and out of the neighbor's driveway, contemplating my next move. It seemed that every home in that neighborhood was empty. Only the street lights were alive, and the houses hid in the dead shadows. I felt as if I truly was the only person on earth.

Something HAD happened. It was no dream.

I told myself that this way of thinking was insane, of course, and that it was just Azzore toying with me again. It was only a matter of time before his divine prank was revealed and he got his laugh. Unless this was no prank, but some malicious tactic to get my attention and demand something more from me, as gods sometimes tend to do.

Unless, also, Azzore was the woman disguised in light but brooding darkness, or even the dragon. Perhaps, it was even all these, and this was the forgotten realm he wandered.

Which conjures the question: who was I to him?

These were all acceptable things to consider, yet they brought me no closer to the truth. I was making myself seem mad. It was time to see where my home was, now. Had I left it behind when I crossed through the shadow into this other place?

Or was I already there?

.....

It was late and I was driving with my windows up. The city streets were empty, which was unusual for a Friday night. I had the music loud as I swerved from lane to lane catching every green light. The earth could've melted within itself right then, and I wouldn't have cared. I had decided that I was where I needed to be and had forgotten about my missing friend and party goers. I was sailing alone, and happy for it. I was a slave to a graffitied mind. I was trying not to notice the city lights exploding up into the night sky and unfolding outward like the fiery wings of a Phoenix when I caught my first red light.

Fate then stepped in, or maybe that fucker Azzore for all I knew.

I was deeply mesmerized by the angelic sounds of Radiohead's *Kid A* album when a luminous shape came into my immediate peripheral. I slowly glanced through my passenger window and saw a popsicle yellow hippie-wagon beside me at the red light. The color was so loud that I remember squinting my eyes and saying aloud, "good weeping God, man!"

My eyes finally adapted nicely to the exuberant van. I noticed suddenly an extraordinarily white hand waving frantically out of the window, possibly needing my attention. My mind was still trying to decipher what I was seeing when a painted face beneath a fiery red and curly wig appeared from the interior darkness of the van into the glow of streetlights, staring at me jovially.

"Jousting Jesus!" I exclaimed as I flinched backward. "It's a fucking clown, man!"

I literally stared with my mouth wide open trying to believe what my eyes were relaying to my brain because it had been apt to deceive me before. I didn't know what was real and what were dreams any more than a lobotomy victim, but upon further scrutiny, I concurred that in fact, it was a clown.

As I stared, and presumably thought, I tried to understand this crazy side-show trip. Just what in Mother Goose's fat-ass was a clown doing on an empty city street at this hour (whatever hour it was)?

Wasn't there a law forbidding this kind of thing? If there wasn't, then shouldn't there be? Something like this could cause a man's mind, in my predicament, to explode.

Why was there no one on the streets? This was very peculiar and sketchy, indeed.

And why was the clown still waving at me maniacally? For some reason, a tremor fear set my teeth on edge. Was this clown in real distress, or was this some plot against me?

I cautiously, and admittedly afraid, leaned to my passenger door and cracked my window.

"What the hell?" I said, catching myself before I began to scream in panic. "I mean, you're not going to try and eat me, are you?"

I had confused it. If this was an insidious rouse to capture me, it now knew that I wasn't falling for it.

But what came next shocked me to the primal core of my manhood. A high-pitched, feminine voice replied, "what? No sweetie, I was just wondering if you could tell me how to get to 171; I'm lost."

What kind of twisted sense did this make? Not only was there a clown staring at me, but it was speaking to me. And it was a goddamned female for Christ's sake! Not only was it a female but it had somewhere to be at this ungodly hour.

As I said, her voice was very high, and I suppose higher than a clown's voice should ever be. She smiled at me amiably. Maybe too amiably, stretching her heavily coated red lips across her white face. I didn't know the proper way to address a female clown, so I just spoke to her the way I would've a male clown, which was exactly the way I would've addressed anyone for that matter.

"Just follow this street, and it's on the left," I said while staring at her blue eyelids that made half-circles around her eyes.

The clown thanked me with a smile and a wave, and it's white face, rosy cheeks, red lips, and blue eyes froze instantly in my conscious and made me want to howl in hilarity. Then just as soon as she had appeared beside me like an angel in the dark, she was gone. The light had turned green, and she had sped away into the empty night in her tiny yellow van.

What sort of mind trap was this?

What had just occurred? Had reality and logic been dismissed by me subconsciously and replaced by lost nocturnal clowns? Female clowns at that. As usual, my mind ran amuck with reasonable questions but generated no answers. Just what was happening here?

Her tail-lights were still visible when I first noticed the trail. The same type of ghostly yellow mist that was left by the space-frog was being emitted by the clown's van. It seemed to be pouring from the tail-pipe like some psychedelic gas preying over the pavement.

"Holy fuck," I thought. Was this wayward clown meant to lead me out of this desolate realm.? Or was this a trick to lead me back to that terrible dragon?

I didn't see where I had much of a choice. I hit the gas promptly and began a new journey for no good reason.

.....

I remember trying to keep the vehicle in the proper lane and Pink Floyd's *Dark Side of the Moon* playing. I know it is perhaps the most mundane tool for enjoying a trip, but it's a very effective one that never becomes obsolete. As the music whipped my soul into submission, I began to wonder curiously about the clown in front of me. I had seen the curly red wig, the white face with the blue paint circling the eyes, the majestic white gloves, and the shockingly red lips. I couldn't remember how big the nose was, or the color; or if she even had one.

Other thoughts began to percolate in my mind. What was her name? Did she have big clown shoes? Could she drive in big clown shoes? If she could, then did that mean the tiny yellow van came equipped with big clown pedals?

I heard the lyrics, "the lunatic is in my head," sway pleasantly from the speakers and laughed wildly to myself. Yes. Yes he is, I thought.

Time was of no concern now; if it even existed anymore. The mescaline held me safe in its arms and kept me warm like some psychedelic incubator. The yellow trail was still strong. I could see it leaving the van and stringing along above the black roadway just ahead of me. I stayed with it, cautious to remain subliminal just in case it was a trap, but close enough to not lose it in case it was my way out. There was some reason it had appeared and yet another reason that I was stuck here. I had to find out whether that reason was in my benefit or not. Besides, I had come too far now. Something inside me told me that this was my way back. After all, I had been washed in the blood on the other side of my shadow; now it was time to return enlightened.

A familiar aroma demanded my attention. I tried to recognize it but couldn't. I began to look around at my surroundings for the first time in a while, for I had been lost in the hypnotic music, and to my confused internal ramblings, for quite some time it seemed. Now I saw all familiar places, but places that I couldn't place at all.

As if straight out of a movie a gigantic goddamn shark with mountains for teeth ready to mush me came from the sky. The image gave me a frigid shiver in my guts and slapped me out of a dumb trance I had been bogged. After only a few seconds I realized the shark was merely a crude gimmick outside of a novelty store by the road. Suddenly, the familiar places and aroma that had been so vague to me were remembered. I was in Panama City Beach, a solid two hours from where my journey had begun.

On the surface, this was very strange. While swinging from this mescaline tree, I had just followed a spirit-like trail emitted supernaturally by a tiny yellow van driven by a lady-clown at some unknown time in the morning in what may or may not have been some alternate realm of my indigenous universe. This seemed even more possible now that I noticed the fact that there were still no cars out and I hadn't seen one since I left the stranger's yard – other than the yellow van.

All of this was strange, yes, but happening nevertheless; and that alone made it even more strange. Which raises the Socratic question: Is it because it is something strange that it is strange? Or because it is strange that it is something strange?

Maybe it is the latter, for it is not because it is something coming to be that it comes to be, but because it comes to be it is something coming to be.

This would become truer than I ever could've thought possible.

The van zigged and zagged, or maybe it was just my perception misleading me, through a pitifully lit neighborhood. I tried not to follow too closely, for paranoia began to set in, and I didn't want to let my guard down in case anything else tried to eat me. It stopped on the side of the street in front of a brick house not too far from the beach. It was dark and the moon was subliminal, but I could hear the waves crashing in the distance. I parked behind it, several feet away and directly in front of a large-mouth bass mailbox, killing the headlights.

The mist between the van and I rose slowly into the air and dissipated intimately like a golden powder in a breeze. There was no movement from the clown for some time, and I began to think, "Fuck! Maybe she had spotted me and was calling the police. Holy Jesus, how will I ever explain myself?" I almost left then – but I didn't. Fate had brought me this far. Fate, or some evil spirit -bitch and what little gas that I had.

Before I could rethink my decision to stay, the van door swung open and a short, pudgy figure hopped out of the driver's seat and stood under the weak lights in the street. I remember the shockingly vivid painted face in the night and the bedazzled suit she wore. There was also glitter; lots of glitter. Some of it even sifted like fairy dust in the air all around her as she moved. She spotted me and then stopped dead in her tracks as our eyes met. There was a vibrant connection that held fast in our gaze; that unexplainable remnant of something lost from before. She waved at me and motioned for me to come to her.

"Madness," I thought. "Pure madness."

Just as the progeny from the sky in the form of a frog had reached out its hand for me to take, so was she. I carefully got out of the car watching the seamless sky for melting stars, but there were none. Under the dull lights of the street, there was something out of sync with what I thought I knew. I could sense that there was something wrong. I can't explain it; only that it was the aura of that weird environment and something that I couldn't see but that I should be seeing.

It was the clown who spoke first.

"Oh wow! You're here for the party too? I didn't know!"

Her voice was sweet and excitable. There was a surge of assurance in it that made me believe that, yes, I did come for the party. Although I had no idea what she was talking about, I couldn't stop visualizing quirky balloon animals and water-shooting flowers; maybe even a puppet show, if we all behaved. Besides, dammit, I come a long way.

"Well hell yes," I said. "Why else would I be here?"

I followed the visually ardent woman up along a narrow walkway through a small plot of grass and onto a moderate sized porch. Umbrellaed by darkness, I saw a studded, sparkling glove reach forth and knock three times on the door. I held my breath anticipating either the horror or glory that awaited on the other side. Within only a few short seconds the porch light flashed on, and the front door opened fully.

In that moment, all that I ever knew to be sane and wonderful in my relatively simple existence withered away and was gone in a matter of only a second. Standing inside the door in a well-lit interior, greeting us with warm smiles and big hair, were three transvestites smiling like super-models.

"Oh Glenda, you finally made it!" All three exclaimed, giggling from excitement. "Oh my goodness! You brought a friend! This is going to be so much fun!"

For the first time in real lighting, I saw the clown beside me morph into a pudgy trannie garnished in piles of make-up. It wasn't some cosmic clown delivering me from a forgotten realm, but a cross-dresser wearing a sparkling onesie, tons of make-up, and a big red wig looking to get laid. Immediately I knew the score and began to laugh uncontrollably. I should've known somehow that this would happen. I should've seen it coming.

I fathomed some excuse, like I had forgotten my cigarettes, and left them to their party. I wanted no part of what was going on behind that door. I had a long trip back home to reel the experience and decide if it had really happened. Of course, it had, but some things are just too fantastical to believe even when you experience them.

.....

It wasn't until the next day that I found out what had happened that night at Kala's. After the frightful encounter with the strange clown, I went to my parent's home and crashed. I awoke that afternoon feeling groggy, my head swollen with pain, and thirsty as hell. The after-effects of an immensely potent trip, such as the one I had, can really mess with your body.

I remember reading somewhere that psychics, and those that display telekinetic powers, suffer greatly in their bodies because of the over-extensive exercise of their mind. Perhaps the same concept applies here. Either way, my spine felt as if it were caught in a beartrap. My stomach churned and ached badly enough to cripple me momentarily. I barely made it to the toilet before shitting all over myself.

Sometimes to experience a certain kind of bliss one must suffer some kind of hell.

After the bathroom, I went straight to the kitchen. Alcoholics prefer a bit of the hair of the dog to help combat a snarling hangover, but for those of us that have pushed our minds and bodies to the outer limits of reality, this is no good. We need only one thing: orange juice.

I poured the juice and gulped it voraciously before pouring another glass. My parents were in the living room watching television. My dad was sprawled in his recliner, and my mom sat on the couch reading a book. As I passed through going back to my room to gather my bearings I could hear the corny theme music for the local channel four news station playing.

The anchorwoman announced the top story as being a crazed man getting arrested the night before. Naturally, I glanced at the screen to make sure it wasn't me she was talking about. To my chagrin, I saw above her head in a little box on the right corner of the screen the familiar face of my friend, Daniel.

Apparently, while I was away trying not get eaten, he had utterly lost his mind – which was hardly a surprise because he was known for this. Sometimes, between the time that I left him swimming in the grass and when I came back from my journey in the stranger's yard, he felt the inclination to perform swan dives and cannonballs into the immaculately shaped shrubs that aligned Kala's house. They were carefully manicured shrubs that made her appear opulent and sophisticated, so for lack of a better way of putting it, she got really pissed off. So pissed, in fact, she hastily went berserk on him like an angry mother taking up for her baby and then prescribed all her fury and rage to everyone else there, forcing them to leave; then leaving herself.

They hadn't been raptured, nor had they been abducted by aliens. Although both were valid probabilities. Most importantly, I was never lost in a secret realm; I had already returned through the door of my shadow when I awoke in the grass.

This only confirmed that Azzore was fucking with me, with his hands on the cosmic strings of fate and chance.

Daniel had wandered off from Kala's house on foot and somehow ended up in the city. He then held up traffic four ways at an intersection while trying to save what he called an "electric fish" from dying in the street. Because the fucker was flipping and flopping too fast, he couldn't apply his grip properly enough to catch it. The more he tried, the harder it became to grab, as if it knew his every move even before he did. It was when he began stripping and using his clothes as a net the motorists became understandably freaked out.

When the police arrived, he must've appeared dangerous and inconsolable, or just an easy target, because they commenced to beat him savagely, breaking his leg. Presumably, they didn't believe that an electric fish was in any danger, or they just didn't care.

I knew not to give him the mescaline from the very beginning, but sometimes it can't be helped. In hindsight, I probably never should've left him alone, but in my defense, if I had never taken that first step out of that yard, there would be no story.

Daniel never made it to boot camp.

CHAPTER 9

A Place of Death, The Beginning of the End

As I finished the story, Jacob sat quietly on a log across from me, watching the flames in the glowing fire-pit dance feverishly. His countenance suggested that he heard none of it. He was lost somewhere else as the others laughed at the story. It was possible, I suppose, that he had heard it but just didn't listen. In the same kind of way that he appeared to have been present there with us, yet not all there at the same time. A piece of him was surely missing.

Or was that just me letting my muddled thoughts conquer my reason?

Helen and Lena's laughter stirred the calmness of the still night. Both sat on the hood of Hess' car smoking cigarettes and occasionally checking their phones for missed calls. This was a time that seemed long ago (but wasn't) when all that cellular phones were used for was making calls. Then, texting was unheard of.

The evil, pungent bastard hadn't jumped on them yet. I could tell this by the normality of their gestures and confident countenance. If it had begun to suffocate their perception, then their demeanors would have been flattened and confused, in a sense. The power of its wonder and force would shine through the windows to their soul.

I, on the other hand, was scratching at the brick wall of lunacy with torn fingernails. From somewhere in the abysmal pit of my mind was some foreign voice screaming at me from within and trying to break free from a sort of cell guarded by my defenseless psyche. It was strange because I could sense it. I could understand and adhere that the will of an unseen and unknown consciousness was trying to shatter my internal being and I was somehow able to subdue it, but its power was building with each waking second. I knew somehow that it was only a matter of time before the invisible demon trying to overthrow my mind broke free from the chains within my drowsy subconscious.

I began to wonder, quietly to myself, if there was another entrance through the shadow on the other side. If I had passed through and returned from the other side, then it would make sense some feral force from where I had been could do the same. It would seem that whatever awaited there beyond the shadow could infiltrate my conscious if the veil had been revealed to be penetrable, either by myself or some wicked potion.

Perhaps knowing this kept me one step ahead of the intruder and allowed me to remain sane for the time being.

As for Jacob, I feared that it was too late. The same type of growling and screaming demon burrowing through my shadow had already broken free and was surely devouring his mind like a rabid beast. He was doing well, I thought, to have not yet plucked out one of his eyes and fed it to either Lena or Helen. I could tell, though, by the livid stare that his mind's eye manifested that he was indeed thinking it.

What the hell was I saying? Why was I consciously narrating Jacob to be some deviant fiend fit for an institution? He had a kinder heart than anyone I knew.

Again, the monster I had introduced to my bloodstream was turning my mind against all that I knew. It was the screaming demon in the deepest, darkest, part of my mind trying to gnaw through the shadow, to consume and infiltrate me permanently. Jacob was only sitting there, quiet perhaps and detached from everything happening, but he was simply just tripping just as I was. He was maybe even holding it together better than me. It was wrong and bastardly of me to assume such nonsense of him.

Lena snapped me from the trance I had fell into by saying, "Hess, it's 7:30. I wanna see the graveyard you told me about."

"What graveyard?" Helen asked as curiosity peaked in her tone.

"Hess told me about some really old graveyard back here." Lena was looking at Hess for some kind of a reply.

Hess cut his eyes at me for approval, and I shrugged my shoulders. "Why not?" I thought. There's hardly anything more chilling than a creepy graveyard in the middle of the woods at night. It would be fun.

"It's just a really old graveyard in those woods," Hess said as he pointed to the western part of the forest that circled the pond.

Which was partly true, but not entirely. Daniel and I had first stumbled upon the graves by accident a couple of years before the Great Mescaline Incident. We happened upon it one day while scouting the woods for a proper place to plant weed and cultivate it. It wasn't until later we learned the story behind them.

"I wanna go see it," Lena declared as she got from the hood of the car. To encourage his participation, she wrapped her arms around Hess and kissed him.

My mind was surprisingly calm. The screaming had silenced, and the paranoia and fear had ebbed.

It made me question why.

Could this be exactly what it wanted? Had it been waiting patiently for this? Had it been destroying my conscious with raucous fits of rage while waiting for this?

Was it there in the belly of darkness at the unkept graveyard that it would overtake us and consume us all?

Internally, I had to shake myself and get a grip of my soul before I cringed it away from body.

The girls stood waiting while Hess retrieved three flashlights from his car. Jacob was still sitting on the log at the fire watching the embers scintillate from the fiery coals up into the sky as he stirred them with the stick. Watching him, I thought that maybe I should step up and announce that it was probably better that we didn't go and that perhaps we should wait until daylight, or at least until we weren't susceptible to some hallucinogenic entity. I still felt that it was my duty to protect him since after all, I had given them the drug that our minds were most likely not evolved well enough to handle.

As I was contemplating this, I heard Hess say, "Jacob, you comin' with us?" When Jacob didn't respond and only stared into the flames, he coaxed, "Come on it'll be fun."

Jacob finally looked away from the fire. Maybe it was my eyes playing tricks on me, but for the first time since we had left Chris' dungeon, he actually seemed stable. His eyes were sane now. There was no dark figure masked within them that I could discern. Surprisingly, he stood up and brushed his pants clean from the dirt and grass clinging to them and in a voice as plain as the color of the moon above us said, "Hell yeah. Let's go."

.....

There was a path that pushed narrowly through the forest that was only visible if you knew where to look because of all the fallen leaves covering the dirt. We walked one behind the other through the dark that was barely penetrated by our flashlights. Limbs reached out across the path like frozen arms; we had to duck most of them but managed to push and bend some from our way. Hess led the way holding a flashlight in one hand and Lena's hand in the other. Lena kept close to him, holding her phone out in front of her for more lighting. Behind her walked Helen with another flashlight, followed by Jacob and then myself with the last light.

Jacob made some fatuous comments like how there were giants sleeping inside of the trees, waiting to awake and rule the earth like they had before. He said he knew this because the trees would bleed when cut. The others laughed at the inanity of his comments, but I didn't. I wondered if he truly believed that giants slumbered in the trees and if maybe he had even seen one.

It forced me to, again, question my sanity.

The girls giggled with apprehension as we drew closer to the site. They still made no indication to me that the rotten shit they had taken had detonated within them yet. By indication, I mean that they didn't yet show signs of extreme catatonia or perverse delusional mayhem, which seemed to be the common factor of this vile mixture. Yes, they seemed to still have their senses, and for that I was thankful. To be in the middle of the forest dealing with humans going primal should be the burden of no man.

Even if that man is somewhat responsible.

All around us, even above and below, was a different kind of night than outside of the woods. The forest imbibed the darkness, accentuating its character. Outside the confinement of the forest, around the calmness of the pond, the moon cast a pale and fragile glow which reflected majestically off the water while refracting into the night, painting the darkness a shade of life. But in the maw of the forest, beneath the lurking arms of trees, the light dies quickly and quietly. Without the flashlights, we may as well have had our eyes closed.

The path winded and twisted about two-hundred yards into the vast woods where it subsequently stopped and opened like a gaping mouth revealing an oval clearing about forty-feet in diameter. There were no trees busting through the earth grabbing for us, only a thick blanket of dead leaves covering the ground and crackling beneath our feet as we walked.

Here there were five tombstones, and only two were still erected while the other three had been pushed from the dirt over the years. It was obvious that they were old, possibly the oldest any of us had ever seen. Even though it had only been a few years since I saw them last, they seemed older still at that moment. Mold discolored spots of the rough stone. They were small, almost half the size of what would suffice as one today. The rough engravings were nearly completely eroded and not at all legible in places. The three upturned tombstones lay strewn like damaged relics of a forgotten time. They were covered with brown, brittle leaves and fallen limbs with only corners of them visible.

Hess knelt in the center of the clearing where two markers were still protruding from the ground. He squinted his eyes, shining his light at one of them. "I can't make out the name on this one. It says, Born 1856 and Died 1864." He trained the light onto the other tombstone still erected. "This one says Tabitha Horn. Born 1858. Died 1864." He managed to speak calmly despite that the young ages of the dead obviously bothered him. He flipped over one that was covered with debris and said, "I can't read anything but the birth on this one, 1856."

"None of them are older than eight years old," I said matter of factly. "And they are all girls."

"So what? All these kids died of some kind of disease?" Lena asked morosely, holding on to Hess as he stood up. Helen was beside her focusing her light at the edge of the clearing into the darkness as if looking for something nervously.

Jacob had been beside me, staring into that same darkness enveloping us. His face and skin had become pale again. Even in the black of the night, I could see the pallor hint of madness washing his complexion. He answered Lena with vague honesty, "They didn't die of disease, but from something much worse." His tone was uncalculated and unmistakably monotonous.

Everyone's eyes were stalking the scene. There was a surreal sense of sorrow dripping from the limbs that grabbed at the air around us. The girls were staring blankly at the small headstones. I could tell by their forlorn gazes that the acid was clawing its way into their minds finally. Hess confirmed my suspicions by saying, "I'm starting to feel that shit." His eyes were wide and excited. His lips were spread in a strange grin.

"Me too," Helen said dryly. Her eyes were like stones atop a scorched earth.

Lena took Hess' light and found Jacob in the dark, his glasses reflecting the light like a mirror and asked him, "what do you mean they died in a worse way than disease? How'd they die?"

There was no expression on his face, his eyes were as black as the night around us, and his hair hung down just above his eyebrows. "They were murdered," he calmly stated.

He was pacing circles around the clearing now. His oddly shaped, skinny frame was like a frail ghost girding us in the shadows. I could hear him breaking; we all could. The silence was magnified in the forbidden depths of the wilderness, and any noise was rampant among us. I wondered just how stable his mind really was. It had seemed that the throes of the possessor's grasp and the malice of its deafening growl had subsided back to whatever world beyond our shadows to remain dormant, but now all of that seemed to be different.

The screamer had never left.

Perhaps I had thought this because, I for one, seemed to be hosting another personality apart from my own standard conscious. The intruder screaming from the void of my mind had broken free and was turning the switches of my internal wiring. It was quiet, which is what was scary. But I could feel it working as it fingered my senses with serrated tentacles. It had what it wanted, and I burned and itched deep inside where I couldn't reach.

These momentary lapses of sanity came and went like waves crashing against a frail wall. How much more could my mind take before it finally snapped? More importantly, how much more could any of the others take?

How long before any one of them began screaming about bloodthirsty demons chewing through their mind?

For the sake of everyone, I had to pull myself together.

Jacob had conjured some uneasiness among everyone. As if being in the forest among abandoned children's graves wasn't enough to manipulate your senses, knowing that they were murdered, now, was more than a little unsettling. I probably should have known this fact would eventually arise. How could it not? I suppose in my stupor and accommodation to the fact helped me to dismiss the relevance.

With a quiver in her voice, Helen asked, "how were they murdered?" The stuff was working on her like a magic spell. Her face was like a stone, expressionless because her drossy mind had refused to regulate her muscles properly. Her eyes were of the same element as the night.

I felt everyone's eyes fall upon me. I knew that I had already been chosen in the silence.

"Go on, tell us," Lena demanded of me. "You can't show us something like this and just leave us hanging."

Maybe this wasn't the best time to be introducing potentially psychotropic ideas. In the back of a functioning part of my mind, I wondered, in all seriousness, if the evil that I had initially sensed enchanting the black liquid was now using me as some psychotomimetic agent to infiltrate their minds, making their shadows penetrable.

Delusional rapping of a paranoid creature is all this is. Right?

"Tell us!" Helen exclaimed, snapping me out of my hypnotic musing.

"Alright, man!" I said, "I will tell you. Jesus."

They gravitated closer to me, their lights bathing me. They gathered and sat before me as if waiting to receive communion. Jacob had stopped pacing and I could see the mold of his thin shadowy frame behind them. I could hear his demon ranting and laughing.

Or maybe it was just my own; it had become nearly impossible to tell.

I began, "this is a story of a man named Lonnie Dade."

CHAPTER 10

Lonnie Dade

Lonnie Dade was born in 1845. His mother pushed him out of her within the wooden walls of a small shack his father had built in the middle of the forest. He was born in literal darkness. His mother and father, Luscia and David, were simple people. They raised pigs and chickens, secluded from everyone and everything.

Once a month, David walked to town pulling a cart of chickens to sell or trade. It was said that Lonnie was mildly retarded, which is why his mother eschewed him from society and other children. It was his father who would give him tiny tastes of the world outside the forest when he took him into town with the chickens.

His mother held onto strict religious convictions. Seventy-five years before, her grandmother had been accused of being a witch for displaying odd and evil behavior. Her mind had become desperately sick, and her children became her victims. She had always been a godly woman, though, and followed the teachings of her church. She poured her beliefs into her children, but over time she began to display violent and depraved mannerisms. One day, the oldest of the four siblings, showed up into town. He was beaten, cut up, and begging for help.

When the constable and preacher arrived, they found Luscia's grandmother naked and emaciated, sitting with her back to a pantry door. The three children, Luscia's mother being one of them, were crying and pleading for help from the other side. She sat in a small puddle of blood holding a knife to her face, slashing the skin just beneath her eye. She was covered with self-inflicted cuts, screaming some strange tongue like a rabid Pentecostal.

Immediately, after seeing her wretched state, the preacher cried out that she was a demon, blaming witchcraft for her possession.

She was burned alive for her malady.

Luscia, fearing her own damnation, didn't want to fall under the same diabolical possession as her grandmother, so she clung to the same religion for protection, though it had condemned her grandmother all those years before.

One evening in 1854, David and Lonnie were hunting not far from their home. David fell out of a tree and into a pack of wild boars and was mauled to death. Lonnie could only watch in horror as they tore his father open. They ate him alive, piece by piece, until they consumed him completely. All that was left were his bloody teeth strewn about in the gore and mud like lost marbles.

Psycho-genetically, the brutal incident would prove to be the catalyst of a monstrous descent from sanity for Lonnie.

It didn't take long at all for Luscia to become unbearably distraught. She began to slip into a lucid and extreme psychosis. For her, reality began to melt away like ice cubes in the palm of your hand. She stopped eating and would fly into hysterical rages without warning, breaking things and hurting herself on purpose. As her mind disintegrated, her belief in God and convictions in faith became more sadistic than anything.

One story tells of her holding her arm elbow deep in a large pot of boiling water while laughing and spitting Bible verses with horrible screams in a fit of wild, fervid madness. The young and confused boy, who had not long before watched his father be mauled and eaten alive, rushed to her wanting to help, but she knocked him away with one powerful kick.

By the time Lonnie was ten the next year, Luscia had become ensnared within a new, more twisted, psychosis to coincide with her religious fantasies. Her mind had split between the two primary roles of her life, mother and wife, isolating one from the other, and prohibiting her from functioning as both simultaneously. Lonnie became the variable of her delusional fantasy becoming whatever she needed him to be for whichever role she was locked into. At any given moment, she would become the eccentric and domineering mother psyche, bashing her misconstrued conceptions of the Bible upon her young son. She seared into his mind that girls were dirty harlots and having anything to do with them would mean being cursed by God. Only a boy's mother could ever be worthy of an exception for God's grace. She taunted Lonnie with Bible scriptures, subjecting him to cruel punishments for not quoting them exactly the way God had said them. He suffered beatings, burns, and verbal lashings that hacked like a dull blade into his mind.

When her personality switched, and a different, more inept, type of delusion manifested to become her reality, Lonnie again became what he needed to be to fulfill the fallacy in her mind.

When the moon appeared each night, she saw him as her husband and would aggressively attempt to seduce him. When his young and innocent flesh wouldn't work the way an adult man's should, she became bestial and frantic, beating him to the point of unconsciousness while spitting obscenities at him as he laid naked in her bed, the same bed that had once been the safest place in the world to him.

The curse of seclusion kept Lonnie from being saved. His screams and the maniacal tantrums of his mother were only heard by the animals in the pens outside. These aberrant acts continued to stain his developing mind throughout his anguished youth.

When he reached puberty and was finally able to substitute adequately as his mother's lover, his defiled mind and body had become so radically warped that only the pain and verbal abuse by her would suffice at getting him aroused. It was the corrosive screams and violent outbursts of clawing and biting and hitting that had become his love for his mother, and he loved to please her more than anything.

When he was sixteen, an incident involving a little girl drastically changed his life forever. He had touched the ten-year-old inappropriately, and when she tried to run away, he bit her on the shoulder. She was terrified and screamed out for help. The men that came beat him to a bloody mess before the sheriff arrived to arrest him. He was held in jail for a few weeks while being treated as poorly as can be imagined, suffering humiliation, and deviant torment from the men hired to guard his cell. The possibility of being hanged loomed over him like a taunting shadow, but he was eventually released only on the strict accordance that he join the Confederate army which was in dire need of cannon fodder. He would die soon, anyway so the Confederacy may as well get some fighting out of him first.

Within only a few weeks he left to fight. It was then that Luscia fell into an even greater disparaging sickness of the mind. She spent most of the daylight hours weeping uncontrollably and the nights wailing savagely at the moon like some dying animal. For her, Lonnie didn't exist only as her son, but as her lover as well. The day he was forced to leave, she lost both of them.

The days reminded her of the light and joy remised while the night awoke a special madness that thrived in the moonlight. Townspeople spoke of hearing aberrant bellows from deep within the constraints of the woods. Everyone believed she had consorted with the devil and that the cries and screams pouring out of her were from her nightly communions. Just like her grandmother, they believed her to be a whore of Satan. It was due to unadulterated fear that no one went into the woods to confront and kill her. The one thing that no one knew, not even Lonnie, was that she was pregnant with his child.

More than two hundred miles away, Lonnie's appearance, and social and mental awkwardness made him easy prey for torturous hazing by the other soldiers. The level of abuse he suffered only slightly more than he had suffered by his mother's hand. At least he loved her. He couldn't find any pleasure to hold onto in their beatings and taunts, except for when they reminded him of her.

War was no place for him, but he adapted to come to love it. He missed his mother and thought of her regularly while missing her bitter and enthralling punishments. He came to adore the pain and cruelty inflicted by the men in his company, all for her. The suffering he witnessed brought a certain peace within himself. He thrived on the blood and pain, believing it was what made him whole as a man. For a while, all that was missing was his mother to touch his dirty parts but that need diminished quickly as he learned from watching the other men that he could do that himself. It wasn't the same though; noting could replace her in his life.

It was said by one soldier that at night, after battles, Lonnie would sit away from the fire, close to the medical tent where the cries of pain and stench of death spilled out into the dark, taking form like a poisonous moon, staring inside at the gore and macabre. He described a longing glint stirring in his eyes as he stared and went onto speculate that Lonnie was even aroused. War was shaping the man Lonnie was born to become more than seeing his father mauled and eaten alive, or even more than the excessively intense mental and physical abuse he suffered. Together, though, all these elements conflated to create the perfect storm between the fickle hemispheres of his mind. No, war was no place for a young man such as Lonnie.

In August 1863, during the Battle of Shiloh in Tennessee, he was shot in the leg. Rain beat down on the raging battle as he lay in the wet field writhing with pain, unable to get up. Bodies piled into hills all around him as he cried in the mud trying to swallow the hurt down. After some time, the Confederates were forced to retreat into the woods, leaving him with the other dying and dead whose final resting place was in the bloodied mud, just as was his father's.

Once the guns stopped sounding and the cannons ceased roaring, the night cast its natural gloom on the battlefield. But it was far from silent. The screams and cries of dying men strangled the thick, warm southern air. At first, the sound of anguish was deafening, but after some time it faded into a quiet death.

Lonnie lay silent, but not dead, with the muscles in his leg shredded by the Minnie ball bullet that tore through it. A part of him wanted to die, but another part of him just wanted to see his mother again. On the damp earth, bleeding in the blood-soaked dirt, he longed for her still and swore he would get back to her.

After two days he was able to climb over the seemingly endless piles of disfigured and mangled bodies rotting under the burning sun. Muffled moans and pleas for death seeped up from the bottoms of piles and through the swarms of flies multiplying from the farthest pits of the killing field, but Lonnie paid no attention. Rather, he focused on blocking the pain until he could crawl to the treeline, where he managed to stand and escape into the forest with a very pronounced limp on his right leg.

By some miracle, he found a Confederate camp where the field surgeon cleaned his properly. Though he refused to have his leg amputated, risking a malicious infection instead, he survived but inherited a horrible limp. It was so pronounced that his foot dragged across the ground like a stiff stick as he walked.

After two years of killing and studying death up close, he returned home. When he arrived home, his gleeful eagerness to see his mother was quickly tarnished. Upon entering the house, he felt the same coldness he had become accustomed to in war. It was the presence of death, a presence that was truly unexplainable, but definite and palpable. He walked into the bedroom and found them.

On the bed beneath a torn and tattered dress, with the aging stains of blood, were the bones of his mother. A deep brown and black, chunky pool of blood had soaked through the quilts and dried on the thin mattress she laid on. Her once beautiful face was now a grinning skull with empty holes where her green eyes had once been. He tried to envision her face with his favorite memory, but couldn't, already the image of the daunting skull replaced what she had been.

Tears all but blinded him as he dragged his dead foot across the room, scuffing the plank floor with his worn boots. Looking upon what used to be her, he had to look away. As he did, he noticed other bones scattered like little sticks on the floor beside the bed. These bones were smaller, hardly formed. The skull rested upside down against the wall in a corner. It was small enough to fit in a large enough hand.

Bemused, he perused the tiny bones, trying to piece together the puzzle the best his muddled and slow mind would allow. There were tooth scratches etched like engravings on many places of many of the small bones. They appeared to have been chewed or gnawed. He sat on the bed after studying the infant's bones and held his mother's in his shaking hands. The same tooth marks from the same sanguinary beast also scarred her bones. He noticed, too, besides her dress having been ripped and torn, that the bed had been clawed at and even chewed in places. At that moment, with the madness incensing his thoughts and sorrow flooding his soul, he realized what had happened. His mother had died giving birth, hence the black puddled stain on the mattress. No one had been there to help his baby as it screamed, begging for nourishment. It lay cold and naked in its mother's drying blood not understanding why no one was helping it. Attracted to its hungry screams, some sort of soul-less beast from the wilderness came and despoiled their flesh from their bones.

Just like his father, Lonnie Dade's only son had been eaten alive.

From that moment, the inanity that was Lonnie longing for his mother became replete with a nefarious spirit. He couldn't satiate the cravings for pain or the powerful lust engrained in him from the horrors of war – the need to inflict what he loved most in the world. He needed to bathe in a plethron of agony and sorrow. He had been baptized in the pain of others and saved by a brutal, murderous mentality.

Eight months had passed since he returned from the war and found his mother and son dead. In that time five young girls had gone missing. It wasn't long after the sixth girl vanished that men from town went looking. They knew exactly where to find him but feared what kind of evil entity hosted the darkness of the woods.

When they came upon the dilapidated shack lurking like some monster under the shadows of the trees, they were met by Lonnie who was covered in blood, dragging his dead leg through the brittle leaves and dirt while talking nonsense about his mother living in the wind and speaking to him in broken tongues.

He was subdued without a struggle, tied-up and left in the dirt while the men searched his home for the girls. Inside the shack resembled a pig pen more than a home. Trash was piled everywhere, chicken bones lay scattered like gravel on the floor, his mother's skeleton was lying in her bed cradling the bones of her baby by her side, and there was a horrible stench as if something had been gutted inside. The sixth missing girl was found bound and gagged in a make-shift cellar beneath the bed he and his mother still shared.

She was soiled and dirty with her own filth and gore, covering her like a veil. The blood still seeped from numerous egregiously sadistic bite wounds spread across her fragile body. It appeared that Lonnie had begun slowly eating her alive, one or two bites at a time.

None of the other children were ever found. Lonnie confessed to crushing their skulls with his boot after they had become too weak from hunger and hurt to scream, or whimper in response to the pain that he inflicted. After killing them, he fed their tiny carcasses to the hogs and chickens in his backyard.

Five headstones were placed near his home where the atrocities occurred. His home that harbored so many frightening secrets was burned to ashes, and he was hung from a tree that yawned like a giant over the girls' memorial. Instead of a burial, he was fed to his hogs. Then they were slaughtered and burned. Burning down the house and leaving the murdered children's memorial in the heart of the forest was the town's way of trying to erase the memory of the lonely miscreant.

But evil has a way of lingering no matter how well it's masked.

DROP

CHAPTER 11

Lost In The Wide Mouth of Darkness

Their faces were stale and lost, and there was a cold silence anchoring the stark atmosphere. In the fettered glow of our flashlights, they seemed like an unfinished painting staring at me with cemented expressions. It was evident that some parasitic foulness had slithered through some space in their minds and took form, burrowing deep within the channels of their subconscious. I remember thinking that maybe it was a bad idea to have told them the story; that maybe their fragile minds were too far gone to accommodate the inception of madness in such a manner.

Jacob continued to detach from us. His mind was operating insufficiently and not in a cool or good way like most acid trips. He stood with his back to us, staring into a vast void of forest lush with darkness. He seemed enchanted by the wind's crooning whisper sifting through the trees, or maybe he was listening to an infant of the dark crying from the night's uterus. I couldn't be sure.

With her eyes strained and widened in the strange glow, Lena said suddenly, "that is a horrible story." Her face was tense and mussed with perplexity. She kept her eyes askew from me and stared afar at nothing at all as she continued, "I don't' even believe it. Why haven't I ever heard it before? Something like that you would think I would've heard before; especially living here."

Twisting her long black hair into knots in front of her face, Helen spoke grimly and assertively saying, "I think you're full of shit."

Hess was sitting on one the headstones smoking a cigarette. He was afflicted with a permanent grin that was lit by straying particles of light from his flashlight pointed at Helen. He seemed to be enjoying his trip so far; his etched smile had turned sadistic. He replied casually, "The story is true. You've never heard it because it is absolutely true."

Both Helen and Lena lowered their brows in disbelief. Neither put any faith in his statement. Even I questioned his sense of reason; he didn't make any sense and lacked the possibility of rational thought in his tone.

He was staring at the sky through the patches in the trees. His gaze, perhaps, was fathoming some unseen spirit slumbering in the clouds. I thought that maybe he would begin to laugh hysterically because of the embroidered smile still tightening his face, but he didn't. Instead, he finished what he was going to say as he slowly trained his eyes back to the girls.

"Because you've never heard it is what makes it true. Tell me, do you think that all of the ridiculous ghost stories that you hear and tell over and over are true?" He paused to pull from the cigarette trapped between his fingers. The quick breath the cherry gasped revealed to me a glimmer of the familiar demon hiding discretely in his eyes.

He exhaled a cloud of smoke that dissipated slowly into the night air and continued, "It's the stories that are kept quiet because of veritable fear that is real. The ones that seep deep into your soul and never leave; that leave an impression and have stained history. People always try to bury true fear, endeavoring to prevent its spread; especially when that fear is at home. Lonnie Dade was real, man, so are his atrocities." He looked around and pointed at the headstones, "these are real." He spoke with a clean coolness that only a strong hallucinogen could produce.

He spoke the truth. It is the secrets that are real. It is the secrets that we should fear.

A gust of wind shook more of the limbs overhead and blew some leaves across the ground, stirring them in a pile. Ancient branches at the highest reaches swayed and cracked in the sky. Somewhere in the distant night one of them broke and crashed to the ground, disrupting the eerie symphony of nature.

Helen bolted to her feet, her eyes bulging and said, "Okay. I'm fucked up, and freaked out. I'm ready to go now."

Tentatively and yet persuasively, I said, "But we just got here. We were just about to dig all five of these fuckers up. Don't you wanna see if they really are empty? You're going to ruin everything. Sit down."

Although I was merely bantering in a feeble attempt to dispel the fear weighting the air, Lena and Helen stared at me with a certain vehemence that suggested that I was maybe the anti-Christ clubbing baby seals on my vacation from aborting fetuses. It was a stare that troubled me greatly.

Thankfully, Hess thought it was funny and laughed, diverting the baleful stares from me.

Jacob was still aloof to anything that could plausibly be perceived as real. Still, in the shadows haunting the clearing, at the edge of where our sanity was barely confined, the darkness beyond spoke to him. He stared at it, his back at us, not moving a muscle.

I thought of calling out to him, or even walking over and speaking, but then thought that maybe I shouldn't after remembering I had heard once that crashing in on someone's trip unexpectedly was like waking a sleepwalker and could endanger them or yourself. At least I thought I had heard that; maybe I hadn't. I convinced myself that I had anyway.

I hadn't noticed that Hess had walked up beside me until he said, "Is he going to be okay?" His voice echoed around in my skull like a hissing breeze for he had startled me quite a bit.

As if in a trance, I answered cryptically, "I'm afraid that the demon has him. It's surely caressing his soul right about now with fiery talons." I spoke with a sedated cadence as I exposed my secret fear.

I felt his psychedelic stare fall upon me, "What the fuck do you mean?"

What did I mean? Did I even mean to say it aloud?

It seemed that I was entertaining my mind again with mono-logical inner ramblings, but now he was staring at me with fat, dilated pupils. His face was stern and seemingly angry.

Was it possible he saw that the demon had ripped my mind asunder?

Was it possible that it really had?

Would I even be aware?

The more that I practiced this monomaniacal pattern, the more copious my paranoia became.

In the background of my thoughts, I heard Hess say sharply, "He's just trippin'. What the holy hell are you sayin'?"

I sensed from him loathing aggression and I recognized it immediately, or at least thought that I had; my perception wasn't ticking properly, and it was difficult to distinguish plausibility.

There was a long silence. I watched Jacob like a shrink probing his patient as he stared into the nothing captivating him. This is what everything had come to: Observing madness take form within my friend, all the while trying to resist its prodding claws.

Before we left the graveyard, I wanted to inquire of Hess if he at all sensed the demon marauding his mind, so that I could study him as he answered. I would know if he had been seduced by it and was lying.

Would that, in turn, make me mad?

I never did ask him. Perhaps my new conscious had persuaded me against it.

.....

As we walked the dark smothered path, everything was like water flowing backward in a dream. Even the wind seemed to be drawn out into a slow vibration pulsating all around us like a living, breathing, organism. Our flashlights burned through the night, bathing the narrow trail with a fine glow. The drug had arrested us all. We walked carefully and attentively; our minds and bodies sensitive to the elements around us. Everyone was silent and stared straight ahead until we reached the pond.

The fire had faded to a low, quiet burn when we returned. Hess began feeding more wood and leaves to the famished flames while the girls sat on a blanket in the warmth's reach. Their gazes were removed from all else but the orange glow of the fire and their eyes were fixated like zombies.

I did feel, though, a requisite desire to say something that could perhaps resuscitate their spirits and inject some reinforcement, for I could see that my story had jaded them. But the same nefarious leech was sapping the validity of my vulnerable perception as well. So, how could I?

Some sort of satanic shriek tore through the forest and then through our bodies, causing me to flinch improperly. Lena and Helen both exasperated stoutly. Lena reached for Hess' arm, but he promptly jerked it away.

"It's just an owl," he stated.

My mind froze for a few seconds. In those moments, I believed that some hideous witch was going to blast through the trees on the beating wings of a monstrous vulture, coaxing us all into a kind of trance long enough to snatch our skin from around our bones. I was bogged down, reeling that possibility and scaring myself, when I noticed something amiss. I had to pull myself together long enough to re-observe everything. I had to be sure that I wasn't really losing my mind. Then it hit me.

Jacob was missing.

I began to think back, trying to remember if he had been with us on the path on our return trip. I had been distracted from everything by the clumsy brushing of the limbs and the gentle humming of the wind. There was a sinking feeling of dread as I was faced with an incredibly tough decision.

First, I felt that I should tell the others, to come together as one and be a team at locating him, but a more resounding impulse saying, "fuck that," created a dilemma within myself. I realized that saying such a thing would only create panic which would then create paranoia.

Looking back now, I can concur that I had been rather terrible at making decisions up to that point. I couldn't even trust myself to think quietly unto my own conscious. That voice in my head was deceiving me and chuckling at me like a fat baby from within.

I had seen how Chris deteriorated from any type of humanity in his smoky and disturbing lair. It had not been my imagination, for he had certainly put a kind of fear within me like that only some putrid creature of the night could inflict. I had glimpsed his fain expression welcoming the demon inside, and yet, I still commenced to dropping that evil dose.

I had also encouraged my naïve friend, ignorant to the way of psychedelics, to drop even as fear and caution already poisoned my mind. Suddenly, I was reminded by myself that I gave this bastard stuff to three others.

In retrospect, I was a total asshole.

Or maybe it was just the lulling sway of that fallen angel's bile cloaked as LSD. I could remember the overwhelming feeling that seeped into me as it summoned me the first time I saw it. I had thought then that I had been silently infiltrated, maybe even bewitched. It isn't improbable to consider that a dark and magical necromancer from a forbidden time, swindling demonic forces through rituals and blasphemous divinations, somehow cast the vile entity into the liquid – which found me. Is it?

Thankfully, Lena broke the haunting silence, and the voice in my head, by asking, "What do you think God's greatest gift to us is?" She spoke like a sleepwalker, in a monotonous and weary tone. "It can be anything." She took her eyes from the sky and found Hess, hoping his eyes would find her, but he was engrossed by the moon's reflection on the pond. Still watching him, though, she said with starry eyes blazing in the fire's glow, "I think it's love."

I wasn't at all ready for philosophical chit-chat, especially with a tripped-out hippie who thought that she was in love. I didn't feel inspired by love or peace or happiness or anything other than the fear which festered in me. My trip was adequately different. My shadow had been pulsating for some time now and was caught between two existing worlds within myself. One, a familiar place with pleasant customs and mundane experiences defining what is me. The other, a wasteland devoid of any commonalities, only fears, and perplexities of self-perception.

But, granted, her inquiry couldn't have come at a better time. I knew that I had to distract them from noticing that Jacob was gone and that he had possibly become one with the darkness creeping around us. Hess began to slip into a more desperate domain apart from us, so I felt that he wouldn't notice. I had to seize the opportunity so quickly I answered Lena, "Love is just suffering. Just ask Jesus for Christ's sake." I paused as my eyes captured the awe of a star shooting across the sky, letting my words float, and then asked rhetorically, "So suffering is God's greatest gift; is that what you're saying?"

I knew this pessimistic take on her comment would incite serious and definite blow-back, but I felt that I was now prepared. I even thought that I could feel the demon tightening its grip on my mind as if excited in some way.

Helen then butted-in with the same droll, hippie-like tone as Lena's, "Love is not suffrage. Love is absolute and everything. It is the greatest gift. There's no doubt." As she spoke, she raised her hands up to the sky as if to capture some unseen thing falling from the stars.

I thought it was the proper time for me to unhinge their whimsical philosophies so I cleared my throat and adjusted my senses, then said piously, "It is definitely suffrage and hardly anything else. To love, you must sacrifice, and with sacrifice, there is inevitably suffering. It's the same principle as war and peace. There can't be peace without some sort of war, whether with words or guns."

"That makes no sense," they both agreed.

"Sure, it does. Just think about it."

I couldn't blame them for not grasping my concept. It was an acquired philosophy. One that took time to manicure and maintain as the truth, like any truth that is once initially revealed.

For them, it was much harder to accept. For years now, they had been subjected to simplicity and optimism, hippie brainwashing. To be told such a thing, by me of all people, was equal to blasphemy in their perspective. Still, I felt that it was my duty, as a human with the slight ability to string thoughts together, to shatter their belief in the power of love because, frankly, I was sick of hearing about it, and of course, to stall them from realizing Jacob was missing.

Lena asked sarcastically, "So if love isn't the greatest gift then what is?"

Still, thinking of Jacob's absence and with the hope of delaying any kind of psychoactive dysfunction, I answered, "Well, if there is a God, the creator and gift giver, or isn't, or was or wasn't, then we surely are blessed and cursed. We're cursed with life and blessed through death."

Both girls curled their lips simultaneously. My dejected concepts seemed to have jaded them, maybe even complicated their own concepts in fact. "So, you believe that death, not love or even life, is the greatest gift," Helen surmised.

"Look at it this way," I began again. "You're kicking and screaming the moment that you're born, and metaphorically, you never stop until you die. Life is full of pain, heartache, and suffering. It's because of love that we experience all three of these in the most extreme of ways."

Lena's eyes slanted as she scoffed, "and?"

"And then you die. And all the pain, heartache, and suffering ends," I calmly stated. "So, it can be construed that when God or whatever left us here, created life and then fucked it repeatedly with immense hardships and suffering, gave death as the solace; the final and greatest gift – peace."

"You are full of shit," Lena snapped. "That makes no sense at all. Death causes more pain and all of those things!" The anger building in her led me to believe that she was beginning to hate me. In life, if you are doing enough to make a hippy-chick truly hate you, you are either doing something extraordinarily right or brutally wrong, there is no in between.

"Tell me then, why does death hurt so much for those left alive?" I asked staring blindly into the fire as it heated my face. The demon was speaking now. It continued, "If you heard that some guy that you never met, living two-hundred miles away had just died in a car wreck, would you be grieved?"

There was no answer, only distant gazes.

"But what if you heard that your father had just died in a car wreck? Would you feel grieved then?"

Helen interrupted, "but that's different."

"Only because love makes the difference," I retorted. "Would there have been the suffering without the love? Would the man's family two-hundred miles away felt any sadness about your dad dying?"

Lean hissed, rolling her eyes, "If there was no death in the first place there would be no pain and hurt. You can't put all that on love that easy."

I paused a moment, not because I didn't know what to say, but because I didn't know exactly how to say it. "Really? That's your rebuttal? That death is the cause of so much hurt and pain?"

"To an extent, yes."

"Let me ask you, then. Do you hurt?"

"Yes. Everyone does. What kind of question is that?"

"Yes. I'm sure you do. And yes, we all do," I said, "and I don't believe that we're dead. Let me ask you this too, then, concerning death and love: if you don't love then does it hurt as bad when you lose something or if someone dies?"

"I don't guess. No," she answered as if she really didn't want to.

"So then tell me," I said, "what causes the hurt – love or death? Wouldn't it be the one that comes first? After all, you did agree that if there was no love, then death wouldn't matter."

Helen stammered, stricken by the ill-effects of the drug, determined to win the debate and said, "That's bullshit! You're just twisting words. The purpose of giving someone a gift is so that they can enjoy it. How can you enjoy death if you're fucking dead? It makes no sense that God, or anybody for that matter, would even consider death a gift. You're insane!"

The acid was all over her like a pit-bull. Her face was tightened, and her eyes were rounded, blackened like the most forlorn point of space. She was indeed tripping, but her mind appeared to be sharp.

Her rebuttal to my point was sound, and this was a good thing, for maybe that terrible creature beyond her shadow hadn't slithered through, yet. I knew that I had had enough time to grow accustomed to its insidious devices and contain it, but I feared that, like Jacob, my friends couldn't decipher its trickery as I had, or thought that I had. Even if it was just allowing me to believe I was in control was better than feeling out of control.

Even as I thought this, I could feel my mind-bending, on the verge of snapping.

Again, it was turning me against myself. I had to be careful; I didn't like the feeling.

She had called me insane. Could I be? Could they see that my mind was being manipulated by some other fiendish conscious? Was it in my eyes?

Or would they just find me out when they realized that Jacob was missing?

Shit! I had forgotten that.

Now I was reminded of how I knew that he had been engulfed by the darkness within his own shadow. This made me pulsate.

I had to find a way to prevent these psychotic ramblings. If I couldn't, then I would be doomed to dwell in a permanent state of paranoia, a psychedelic hell at least, until the bastard shit wore off.

I had to regain control. Sanity was at stake here. I had to keep talking.

Even if it was the demon, it felt like me, and that was soothing enough.

"Now, where was I?" I thought and gazed through the fire at Helen. The flames between us danced like enthralled lovers, making her in the backdrop seem like an ardent silhouette of a star fervently breathing. I had gathered myself enough to finish, "Death is the perfect solution for an imperfect existence. If existence was perfect, then we wouldn't suffer. For whatever reason life wasn't given to us to be lived in perfection, so we get temporary satisfactions that seem to be gifts, such as love, but are just entangled with the imperfections. Imperfections such as pain, heartache, and suffering which all come in the same package because it is bundled within life. So, the only thing perfect and the only truly great gift is death." I said the last sentence softly, almost speaking directly to the flames.

"You're just a morbid psycho," Lena declared. "It's not a gift."

I lit a cigarette and exhaled the beautiful smoke from my lungs then said with the calmness of a cold-blooded killer, "If it's not a gift then why is it the only thing that becomes us all?"

Helen spoke loudly again, "That's not true. What about life? We are all given life."

"Not everyone. Think of the still-born babies and then say that. Were they given life? No, they were given death and never had to suffer."

Lena and Helen both huffed together. They both appeared to want to say something but didn't know what. I smoked my cigarette and watched them fight against their reason. My words had been uncomfortable for their minds to accept and they were squirming internally. If anything, I was pleased with myself for forcing them to question their hippy reluctance to the truth.

I smoked my cigarette, laughing quietly within.

CHAPTER 12

One More Song

As Hess studied the pond and its majestic calmness, and the girls laid in the grass watching the stars, I found myself thinking of Jacob and how he was possibly lost somewhere in the darkness. I suppose it was possible he was where he wanted to be. I had seen his face, the way it was emotionless and bland, and what I thought that I saw was a longing for something else. I could hear that distant wail in my mind that was not my own and could assume, gleaning from my own experience, what it was that he was experiencing. It could've been nothing, of course, except my own mind projecting a false perception of struggle.

With all honesty, at that time, it was unclear to whether some pestiferous agent combing through his neuro-wiring had induced some catastrophe within him or if he was just content in his trip somewhere in the woods. After all, the echoing of that demonic scream still ran laps in my mind, reminding me that I had nearly become lost in the ruins of that dark cave of paranoia and was still trying to escape.

My gut was wanting me to believe that he wasn't lost out there somewhere, except in his own mind, and just enjoying the darkness, perhaps even watching the fire from afar in the woods. My mind, on the other hand, was wanting me to believe that he had been taken and we would probably never see him again.

I waited, hoping that he would come stumbling out the forest at any moment so that I wouldn't have to go looking and create a collage of paranoia among my friends when they realize his absence.

At the graveyard, it had appeared to me that depravity was swelling in his pupils. The way he peered into the night was abnormal, but then is anything ever normal tripping. I had convinced myself there that the same type of demon crawling around in my head was doing the same within him and that feeling hadn't passed. The most concerning part of everything happening that wouldn't let my worry-free, was that his mind was a virgin to the drug.

How could he ever fight off such a beast if I was struggling myself?

My mind's eye began to re-visualize the past. Memories of him flooded my thoughts, but a certain one stood out that I couldn't let go of. I would be completely remiss if I didn't share now.

.....

It was 1998, late in the night during the month of January. The southeastern winters in Threscia are defined mainly by a seeping kind of cold that wraps you before it soaks in. It's a damp cold that doesn't nip at you, but rather sinks its teeth in your skin to infiltrate your bones. The wind comes barreling off the gulf, slapping at you with damp whips that claw at your skin.

It was during the dull moments in the aftermath of a large party hosted by a guy named Darren at his parent's house. I remember that two kegs had been sucked dry and that there were seven of us lone survivors remaining, still trying to float a third. We all sat huddled like hobos around a raging fire that oozed out heat for us, only to be nullified quickly by the violent and brisk gusts of frozen wind ripping through the flames.

There was Darren, Kyle, Steven, Kevin, Hess, Jacob, and myself, all talking and drinking. Being young and drunk gave us the valor to withstand the incredible cold tugging at our flesh.

I had to piss and I debated if I could manage standing up properly without falling face first into the flames. I was in the stupor state of drunkenness. That inevitable stage that creeps upon you maliciously, causing your mouth to gape as if you are about to go into some slow song, but instead drool pathetically as you slip carelessly into full retard-mode just before passing out. The only thing keeping me awake was the cold.

We were in the quiet country surrounded by fields. A single isolated road that bled away from an obscure county road was the only way in or out where we were.

Someone, Kyle was in the middle of a crude joke that was probably prohibited in some parts of the country. In the darkness where the road hid, a glowing set of white and red eyes streaked by. To everyone by the campfire, it was evident that the car was going much too fast to handle the curve that lay in waiting ahead. Then, the sound of barking tires skating on the road, followed by the rolling thunder of metal on pavement and crashing glass pulverized the silenced of the night. The floating glow of headlights disappeared abruptly.

A symphony of disoriented 'what the fucks' arose in unison from us as we scrambled about, shaken by the unexpected commotion. The functioning body's capability to shift from drunken paralysis to revitalized machine keen and spry in unexplainable. It was the shocking surge of adrenaline that wrecked the bus already swerving in my mind, bringing it to a sudden and needed halt.

Before I could grasp what was happening, I was on the back of an ATV zooming through a field towards the sound of the crash. Kyle was driving. His arms were outstretched, and his hands were gripped tight on the steering bars. I tried to guard my exposed face from the wet lashing of the brutal wind behind his body, but it didn't work; it found me no matter where I hid. The cold was suffocating, even with the adrenaline still fueling me.

The crash site was quite remarkable when we arrived. At racing speed, a Ford Mustang had tried to round a curve and failed. It sat like an exhausted and beaten fighter, upright on four blasted out tires and its metal crunched and wrinkled. The hood was caved-in from where it had flipped. It had tumbled over maybe twice before finally slamming into a large oak tree a dozen, or so, feet off the road. Dust sill lingered like tiny phantoms in the red glow of the tail-lights, and shattered bits of glass sparkled like diamonds in the grass.

When the ATV stopped, I jumped off with my mind in a haze of confusion and excitement. Immediately, I saw that the driver had gotten out of the car, and while on his hands and knees he heaved blood like a fountain from his mouth. When he looked up at us approaching, I saw that he had a deep cut just above the bridge of his nose. Blood had spread and covered his entire nose, trailing down the sides of his nostrils like red rivers, snaking over his lips and mouth, staining his skin like the warpaint of some ancient Indian. It spilled more profusely out of his mouth, though, slurping down his chin in grotesque gushes and puddling on the ground between his hands.

In the headlights of the ATV, he appeared disoriented and fragile in his sanity. He was staring at us in what resembled blind rage as if we were barbaric villains that had come to ransack his village and rape his women. Perhaps the roaring purr of the ATV's engine upon our arrival was far too much for his scattered paranoia to bear.

Things seemed to then get worse. He began thrashing his hands about as if a horde of bees were imaginatively swarming around him. He produced strange, irritable, sounds from his throat that stopped us in our tracks only feet from him. We were all afraid to touch him. He seemed feral and dangerous. The guttural shrills were like the nonsensical utterances of a child wanting to communicate with civilization for the first time, although having been raised by coyotes in the wild. All this time, he continued to gush and salivate blood from his mouth like a bulimic vampire.

I heard the distant, rattling hum, of another ATV piercing through the frigid wind, although now I was focusing more on the person bleeding and now pleading on his knees something inaudible and incomprehensible. As I inched closer to him, I realized that he was far more injured than I initially believed.

I heard Kyle from somewhere close behind me say, "don't touch him, man. Wait for help."

"Holy shit!" I nearly screamed. "He's really hurt!"

He had bitten off his own tongue, hence the awkward gurgling and crying. The shock of it was paralyzing his eyes into a terrified stare. They gazed traumatically at me; frozen in fear, not seeing. It was the kind of fear that could never be expressed or understood by anyone that has never bitten their own tongue off.

I heard wheels skidding on the pavement as Kevin locked the brakes and came to a stop with Jacob on the back.

"Holy Christ, man! Is he okay?" I heard Kevin ask as they both approached behind me, "We called 911."

Jacob shot past me without uttering a word. His eyes were on the driver and nothing else. "Hey man," he said calmly, "it's gonna be okay. Let me see."

"Dude don't touch him!" I heard Kyle demand again.

Jacob ignored Kyle's plea as he knelt and put his left hand on the driver's back trying to coax him to soft, even breaths. The wet croaking sounds he made as he tried to shriek fell to a slithering hiss as he calmed down. Blood still drained from his chin into an expanding puddle in the grass. Jacob wore a heavy Troy University sweat-shirt over another layer of long-sleeved clothing and removed it quickly, handing it to the bleeding driver to hold in his mouth.

"Can you stand?" he asked him as he hinted at helping him up.

Carefully, the driver stood, holding the sweatshirt to his mouth, I could see it in dim headlights stiffening with slow freezing blood. I helped Jacob ease him onto the dry grass by Kevin's ATV.

"Kevin, go to the end of the road and make sure the ambulance gets here." Jacob's voice carried defiantly in the shredding gusts of wind. There was a glint of concern, yet assurance, glowing in his face. I couldn't help but wonder that if saving this person would in some way appease the uneasiness tightening around his soul after losing his mother at a young age.

From near the car, Kyle yelled, "There's someone in here!"

As Kevin disappeared in the grasp of the night with the driver, Jacob rushed to the car. I followed curiously behind, oblivious to everything, and squatted at the driver's side window. I peered through the shattered glass. I could see beer bottles strewn about in disarray, and some busted in shards while others remained intact. Cubes of ice were scattered about in the seats and floorboards. A silver cooler had been flung around inside and rested awkwardly upside down on top of the driver's seat headrest. A mess of napkins, candy wrappers, a fast food bag, and cups littered the interior as if it were some trailer park dump site.

There was blood everywhere. It had puddled in the driver seat and was dripping from the steering wheel. A thin spray of it had lightly coated the dashboard. Lying on the floorboard, like a slug sticky with blood and peppered with dirt, was the severed tongue.

In the passenger seat, still strapped in the seatbelt, was a young brunette woman. She was probably around twenty-one years old and was wearing a black leather jacket that was opened revealing a pink low-cut, V-neck shirt underneath and jeans with black boots overlapped with white, fluffy wool at the ankles. Ice from the cooler had rained on her and spread out sporadically. The cubes were positioned picturesquely on her body. Pieces were tucked astray in the dark curls of her hair glistening like silver eyes in the night, while a few had fallen free and were slowly melting away against the golden-tanned skin between her breasts.

A long, isosceles shaped piece of glass had torn her skin, through her veins and muscles in the side of her neck and was jutted out grotesquely. Blood both fell and sprayed. It fell in thick, uneven, sheets down her throat, soaking her shoulders and lap. It sprayed in a systematical series of short spurts in multi-directions, depressurizing into a fine red-mist finally before starting over again in the macabre pattern. Heavy gushes of it leaked over the shard of glass penetrating her and covered it in a thick red veil. It dripped off the jagged edges like the drool from a rabid dog's jaws.

The stench from a mixture of blood and the spilled beer turned my stomach. I had to look away often and inhale the cold air to settle my stomach. The tongue-less driver behind me, gurgling in pain, only added to the distress.

The ice bedazzling the interior of the Mustang resonates within my memory because in the wide glow from the headlights of the ATV, I could see that they were painted with thick coats of her blood. The extreme cold was rapidly dropping the temperature of it, and because of this, instead of the cubes melting away, they instead imbibed it like transparent leeches. The ice cubes, draped with blood, were everywhere soaking in the light that was pushing through the night. The overcast of red-gloom projected by the stained and illuminated cubes washed the entire interior of the broken car. It was as if I were staring into some glistening, morbid, cold inferno.

She took small, short, and troubled breaths as if the oxygen were too painful to take in. I imagined her as if a fish stranded on the bank of a pond listlessly sucking at useless air. Her eyes peered wide and frozen at the night through the shattered windshield. I could sense that she was incoherent to reality. It was as if she could see some infinitesimal part of her afterlife expanding greater with every relative second before her.

"The ambulance better fucking hurry, man," I said to anyone listening. "She's losing a lot of blood." I couldn't help but feel a kind of veritable fear for her that seized control of every sense I manipulated to try and understand the reality of what was happening. I had never been there at the moment that someone died. The nature of it all disturbed me in ways that, to this day, reverberate dark and helpless feelings within.

Jacob stood at the passenger's window looking in on her as she bled out. Despite his scrawny and frail physique, he struggled but managed to pry the door open. Loose fragments of glass fell behind the door panel and rang tiny dings as a scattering wave of pangs rolled around inside.

"It's going to be okay. Okay," he whispered to her confidently and embracing. Everything in my mind told me that she could hear him, although her stagnant stare remained fixed on the night. He took her by her bloodied hand and squeezed it lightly. With his left hand, he brushed her forehead as blood spat from her wound and splattered his right hand that cuddled hers in her soaked lap. He never flinched or let go.

"Would you like for me to sing?" he asked gently. He searched her eyes, perhaps for some hint of adherence. Whether he received it or not, he began to sing, all the same, tracing his fingers along her forehead and rubbing behind her small knuckles with his other hand. He sang in a beautifully tortured voice that I never knew he had.

"Come to the forest, and I'll show you pain.
I'll show you loss.
Come to the meadow, that's been washed away.
There's no one home.
A face in a dream. It was you. It was you.
A face in a dream. It was you. It was you.
Come to the river, and I'll show you scars.
Where it all ran dry.
Come to the garden, where it's withered inside.
It all has died.
A face in a dream. It was you. It was you.
A face in a dream. It was you. It was you."

In that long and agonizing, yet beautiful moment, empathy blossomed like a poisonous rose and infected me. I suddenly felt the pain that he must've felt while waiting and watching helplessly as his mother faded away and died. The intolerable infliction that surged like venom in his heart overtook me in one stout and cold wave of hurt. I knew that although this was some stranger bleeding to death in his arms, that in his mind he was holding his mother one last time; singing to her all he had felt all those years since he last saw her.

In the resonating wake of the verse he sang, her body stopped twitching for air and the blood stopped spraying from the gape in her neck. Just before her soul drifted to the unknown and her mind fell asleep forever, a single tear slipped down her cheek. Jacob let go of her hand and closed her eyes. He bowed his head, keeping his hand pressed against her forehead, and said a quiet prayer. When he looked up at me, I saw the water welling in his eyes.

He never talked of that night again. Even when the events were rehashed by those that were there, I was the only one that witnessed what he did, so it was never mentioned.

CHAPTER 13

Return of the Beast: Waves of Badness

My reflection of the past was interrupted by Hess. He came over to the fire and threw more wood into it. He ran his hand across his head, through his short hair, rather slowly and began to look around curiously. He turned to me and asked dubiously, "Where the hell is Jacob?"

Fuck! I thought. This was it. The end. Sanity would surely fall now.

Everyone looked around suspiciously, stabbing at one another with uncertain glances. The fire was raging now that Hess had fed it more wood to devour and every face was washed with is brilliant glare. Just as I had feared it would happen, every face seemed to be stricken with panic. Lena and Helen stood to their feet and monitored the darkness. They mulled the possibilities as they tried deciphering what was happening. Perhaps they were even thinking, as I was, and feared the darkness had gobbled him up like a speck of light near a black hole. There was no way of knowing what that nasty demon was sweetly coaxing into their minds. They may have even suspected that sleeping giants within the trees had ripped him apart.

"Where did he go?" Lena asked disquietly. Her eyes floated to Hess who was glowering intently at the darkness beyond us.

"Stop playing around, Jacob!" he yelled incriminatingly. His abrasive tone boggled my nerves and parts of my flimsy mind flinched. While concern and worry flooded everyone else, anger and suspicion seemed to have overtaken him.

"Did he even leave the graveyard?" Helen asked no one in particular, still watching the shadows for movement. “I don't remember even seeing him since we got back."

"I don't know," I said. "He could've. I really don't remember, man."

In one incredibly dirty gangbang: panic, paranoia, fear, and confusion impregnated the atmosphere just as I had foreseen. Helen and Lena were at odds in agreement. Helen swore that he had been present on the path with us, while Lena was adamant that we had abandoned him at the gravesite. Both were very influential, but I could neither make up my mind or convince myself even to try. I was swirling in the fog the predicament induced. I could ascertain, though, fear brooding.

Hess was completely sold on the possibility that he was screwing with us. He went so far as driving his car around the pond and the entire clearing, shining his lights everywhere to expose him hiding. He was nowhere to be seen.

We called out to him. The girls were screaming his name for literally ten minutes, stopping in only short intervals to listen for a response.

Nothing.

Not even a bug farted in the silence.

What had happened?

It was all too confusing. I was in no shape to handle anything, let alone a goddamn disappearance.

Hess was standing with his back to us and the fire, facing the pond again. I'm not sure if he was speaking to himself or to us, but softly and yet sternly he said, "there's no way he doesn't hear us. He's fucking with us." He then turned and faced us with dull, crazy eyes that glared in the fire like shards of gold. "He's out there fucking with us!" He was pointing to a generalized area that we understood to be anywhere in the vast forest.

I didn't believe him, nor did I really think he ever left the graveyard. My thoughts traversed many possibilities, but the one most plausible to me was that as he was staring into, and hearing, the darkness he had allowed something in. Not him himself, though, but the demon which had materialized through his shadow conscious and then invited something from those masqueraded depths beyond the graves. It had selfishly welcomed the dark, and his body was merely an expendable vessel, and his mind was the sacred victim.

I knew this but didn't understand how I knew just as I knew from the beginning that the acid was cursed. Just as I somehow knew that the portal of the shadow within us all opened both ways and that if we could pass through then so could some unknown being lying listlessly and patient beyond the other side; and only God knew what that bastard was capable of.

I kept my thoughts locked away tight for I didn't want to sound crazy. Things were crazy enough now as they were. Besides, I didn't want to upset the demon stirring within the others.

As I pondered, I felt as though it was I losing my mind.

It seemed impossible to stay calm with paranoia freezing the air around us. Helen grabbed at her lower lip and took a sharp breath into her lungs saying, "What if he's out there?"

Lena was shaking her head with her eyes fixed upon the pond, "Oh my God. I don't want to even think about that. That would be horrible. It is horrible."

Hess was stalking around the campsite. His anger seemed to throb and fester from within him by the minute. I understood him, though. This is what I feared most: His rage.

Maybe I was just losing it, after all, I had thought so on more than one occasion thus far.

"He's not fucking lost," Hess snapped. "Stop trying to freak everybody out!"

Helen raised her eyes at him. It had appeared that he had spoken harshly, but perhaps, like myself, she thought that she was misconstruing actuality because she sheepishly apologized to him.

He continued, "He can't be lost. Even if he did somehow get separated from us, he would be able to see the fucking fire. Or hear us for Christ's sake." His tone was defensive and mean. I still wasn't at all sure why.

As belligerent as he sounded, he did have a point. Besides, stomping around in the woods at night with a head soaked with acid may have been fun any other time, but not this night. Even I could see that.

"You're right," I said. "There's no way we'll ever find him even if he isn't lost. Besides I'm too ripped to be lost out there myself."

I could see the apprehension melting from their troubled stares to their stone faces. They didn't want to go into the woods any more than Hess and I did, but they didn't want to sit idly by leaving him out there alone either. After some discussion, we all, with the exception of Hess, agreed that if he wasn't back after an hour, we would go look for him. I had tentatively agreed to hope that it would never come to that and he would just come strolling out of the forest laughing, calling us all dumb-fucks for worrying.

The atmosphere was heavy with fear, and I could feel it dripping like cold rain on us. We all knew that something terrible had happened or was going to happen. Even Hess knew this, I think. The ominous foreshadowing permeated the setting we occupied with destined travesty. Hess lurked around the outer reaches of the light from the fire, studying the darkness for signs of Jacob. The girls were quiet, possibly thinking of Jacob and the horrors he must be facing alone in the woods.

I had been in a kind of catatonic stupor. Fire always made me lazy while tripping, and this time seemed to be magnified quite a bit. I was staring at nothing, mostly just thinking and listening to Lena and Helen babble endlessly when movement from the sky caught my eye. Like in the stranger's yard, the stars began to slide around in the sky like raindrops on a windshield, beginning to converge together in a strange alignment. They seemed to form sharp and soul-less eyes curved like a blade in their corners. They were parallel to each other glowering downward with a mystical vehemence at me. They didn't move or vary in any kind of way, which was chilling, like an ancient gothic painting. They only held still in the black void above us all.

In the instance of a single blink, the image painted in the night changed. Beneath the dazzling eyes manifested a sneering grin as the stars consistently moved together to form it. It cut through a thin smoke colored cloud and stretched across the sky for what appeared to be miles. It was etched meticulously to coincide immaculately with the staring eyes.

Between the cunning smile and slashing eyes, as if by intelligent design, other stars began to gravitate to each other. They swam like silvery minnows in a black pond and came together forming two pitted nostrils that seemed to breathe balefully as I stared, petrified within. The image had turned my blood cold, and the demon inside me howled, mocking my fear. The sparkling white radiance of the stars began to shift to a more sinister blood-red hue.

I knew the snarling features from my past. I knew them from the night I had entered the consciousness of that sinister woman after climbing through the shadow. The same face that was now an image in the night sky was the same that had been haunting me subconsciously for months while tarnishing my dreams and assailing my thoughts. It was the progeny of her, reborn before my eyes in the bile and blood. It was a great yellow dragon who had sniffed out my flesh and found me. Its bold yellow complexion had evolved into a sanguineous appearance. The bloody glint from the converged stars cast a hideous glow that spread like red smoke throughout the empty space inside the fiendish beast's outline, coloring in its most prevalent features.

And it watched me. Only me.

With instant furiousness, ripples of fear overwhelmed me. My muscles completely relented, and my entire body weighed a ton on my bones. I couldn't move and could hardly breathe. I could only be fed upon by its devouring gaze.

My mind echoed for answers, but only fathomed more questions.

What did this mean? Had the demon summoned it here for some prophetic outcome?

Or was this the demon?

Like some child alone in his bedroom haunted by the ravenous shadows on the wall, I closed my eyes to hide from the stalker in the sky. I had to ignore its terrible eyes and serrated grin.

"Ignore it, and it will just go away," I thought.

"Oh my God!"

I heard Lena's voice from what I imagined was a far-off distance beyond the much closer shrill of my own inner one. Afraid of what I might find, I opened my eyes slowly and peeked into the black sky. Her tone was in that of shock and I whole-heartedly expected to find her chewed corpse scattered around me in bloody pieces.

But there was nothing, no heavenly dragon glowering like an angelic predator. And, most importantly, there were no dead bodies soaked in blood, muddying the soil.

"You'll never believe this," Lena said. Her eyes were terrified and her voice almost unbearably shaky. She was exhausted by her intense trip, but her emotions were on high alert status. She continued, "I am tripping so hard right now. This can't be true."

"What the hell is it?" I barked, now she had my emotions on high alert. I had almost been eaten just seconds before and now this – how could she?

She held her phone out towards us. Hess and Helen moved closer; their eyes were tired and worrisome. Their trips had been chipping away at them as well.

"You know that guy, Chris; the weird guy you guys, hang out with sometimes?"

I nodded, "What is it?"

"Laura just told me that he's dead."

DROP

CHAPTER 14

Forty-Six & Two

The two racially challenged idiots, Mark and Murray, had shown up at Chris' house unexpected, hoping to score some acid. I'm sure they must have found him sideways from reality just as I had earlier that day, sweating in his drab living room, perhaps even ranting under his breath like he was apt to do. I could only speculate, but I can imagine how their sudden and unforeseen presence engaged some kind of primordial switch that unfastened his demon's restraints.

One of them, or perhaps even both, probably said something like, "Wat up cuz?" or some sort of hip-verbiage such as that, jolting him from his inept conscious dreaming.

Chris possessed a kind of stare that could speak in violent and rabid tongues as it cut directly through you. No doubt that as his mind was abruptly breaking, he was slicing them in half with it. Their words would have meant nothing to him. The noises they hissed were verboten to the demon shedding its skin within him.

I can picture Chris cutting them in two with his serpent eyes from across the room in the remarkable gloom. I can see his expression crazed, and taunting obscured only slightly by the heavy haze of cigarette smoke absorbing the glow from the television screen. I could hear the grunting and roaring of fiendish zombies reverberating in the otherwise silent room as they ripped and tore the flesh from the screaming victims on the television.

Any kind of verbal relations with him at this point would have only led to non sequitur ramblings off his feigned tongue. Most definitely, the demon already had ample amount of time to subdue him entirely and contaminate his psyche with its parasitic germ, tapping maliciously into whatever depravity was already rooted within him and pulling it free.

If deviance and evil secretly lurked within anyone that I knew, unexposed and anonymous, it would be inside Chris. So, when I heard that he had gone bestial and butchered two people I wasn't surprised even a little. I had been getting to know the demon and had become acquainted with its consistent plots to overthrow and collapse my sanity altogether. Conscientiously, I had been diligent enough to fight against it, keeping it locked away in a subconscious prison.

Yet the screams wailing from the pit of my mind were getting very close to becoming my own. Oppositely, ever since I had first met Chris, his mind-state had been fucked. Was he capable of murder? I never thought so; only that he was strange. Yet, earlier that day when I saw him he had seemed to be in some invisible and insidious womb, or cocoon even. Only when he awoke transformed, he had shed the gauzy shell of sanity and was one with his inner-shadow.

All that he needed was a slight push to fall from reality completely.

It was around 9:00 that night when Sheriff Kahn got the call concerning loud screams emerging from Chris' home. He and his deputy, Chase, arrived and entered oblivious to the macabre awaiting inside. Immediately, they were struck by an unbearable carrion-like odor that crammed down into their guts as if they had swallowed a foul spirit.

In the living room, they found two bloody bodies. Each of them stabbed dozens of times in no particular pattern. It was the immaculately grim portrait of madness and ebullition. The syrupy blood seeping into the carpet seemed to be the blackest color conceivable in the dark room lit by only the savage zombie film playing on the television.

One body was lying face down on its belly. It had fallen across the table in front of the couch, crashing onto an ant-farm, incidentally breaking it. It was Mark's body, the upper half of which was numbly hanging over the table with his face mashed to the shag carpet as if he were sipping the congealing pools of blood soaking it. Shards of glass and scattered blood-drenched mounds of dirt decorated the floor and table. What looked like millions of wired ants marched endlessly through the blood which was still oozing gently from the fresh wounds. His eyes were open and an expression of fleeting terror still gripped his face which was half submerged in a maroon sludge.

The ants were scurrying around in a confused panic on his scalp, pacing in out of his thick hair-line, dancing down his forehead. They ran across his soul-less eyes down to the crevices of his bluish, cracking lips. There was a deep hole in the side of his neck, just below his ear, breathing blood in dull streams stroking their way down to the carpet. It pulsated eagerly from the hundreds of curious ants bathing in the torn flesh.

A thin, elongated, line of them stretched from his body marching like revved soldiers down his right arm and off his fingertips across the grisly floor and was parading around like jovial spirits on the second body a few feet away. Murray lay on his back in a spreading sheet of blood on the floor. A bone-handled knife was crudely jammed in his left eye, on the opposite side his right eye had been removed roughly. His throat hadn't been sliced, but rather gouged at several times until eventually, it had just burst inside out. An array of stringy tendons and muscles were splayed out like messy, limp tentacles. The ants bathed like angels in the glory of God's light within the exuberance of gore and blood.

Further down his body, his entire torso had been kneaded and sliced to the point at which there were no holes to observe individually, but rather just one large gaping wound swirling with waves of busy ants. The distinct smell of death filled the room, but an odor even fouler swam down the hallway lingering menacingly among the corpses. The pungency of the stench overshadowed the ripe aroma of death seeping from the wounds of the bodies. It was a more bile smell that carried with it an aura of evil and depravity that was unmistakable. The hallway from which it escaped was dark, except for only an ominous glow barely breathing through the cracks of a closed door on the right side.

Sheriff Kahn and Chase trained their lights down the narrow gullet harboring the fetid stench. With their guns drawn in front of them, they approached the door that leaked the faint glow from the exposed spaces. Thinking that he was prepared for whatever waited for him on the other side, Sheriff Kahn carefully opened it while announcing himself. It creaked like the lid to a tomb as it swung open revealing a ghostly scene that seemed too graphic to really be authentic.

From the ceiling, hung seven cat carcasses which were tied to the rafters by string by their tails. They dangled, lifeless, like some macabre Halloween decorations. All but the fur on their tails had been skinned so that the slimy muscles and sheets of yellow flesh still dripped blood onto the tile floor. Their heads had been severed and strategically nailed through the eyes sockets to the wall forming a rudimentary circle. Their tongues hung lazily from their frozen death grins. Floating lethargically in the toilet bowl were all four-teen eyes with loose, stringy flesh dragging behind them like decorative streamers. The sink was stained red, puddled with blood and bits of fatty flesh from where the felines had been hacked and skinned.

"Well, here are all the missing cats," Chase said.

In the tub, half-filled with blood and shit, lay Chris. He was naked, holding a sharp blade with a loose death grip in his right hand. His left arm was gashed open from his wrist to the fold of his elbow. His eyes were widened and fearless; his mouth was stuck with the same maniacal grin that he had when I left him earlier that day.

He was dead. The demon had taken every bit of him and had left nothing for spoil. First, it was his mind and then it was his life. His shadow had bordered a dark and dangerous dimension. It was a place that his mind had no chance or even hoped to harbor safely and even after his demise fragments of its existence were left behind to contaminate ours.

Perhaps we each possess disparate shadows within ourselves that are the empty space between incongruous other-worlds that are either tapped into or tapped upon in some way. If this is so, then these worlds can be strange, abstract, good, or evil.

After making certain that the body in the tub was indeed dead, Sheriff Kahn stood up and looked in the mirror above the blood-stained sink. He had been so disgusted and overtaken by the grisly remnants left in it, he hadn't noticed the mirror. Masking the reflection of his own face was a jaggedly depicted caricature of an open-mouthed demon drawn in blood. Below it, uncouthly written, was the message, *'forty-six & two.'*

CHAPTER 15

The Sound That Broke Sanity

The details of what Chris had done were vague after hearing them. Although the names of the two he had murdered weren't disclosed to us that night by Lena, I knew it had to be Mark and Murray. Even though I had been aware of the malady afflicting Chris' mind I had still sent them there. Not only did I sense the creeping sickness, but I had also felt it, and it had scared the piss out of me. Still, for reasons obscured from me, I sent them there – and I felt a little bad. I was responsible for their deaths.

In all actuality, there was no way that I could've known I was sending them to their demise. But I couldn't help but wonder if the demon had subtly pushed me to direct them there.

Was it that clever and persuasive to have manipulated my behavior? Could it have known what was going to happen and used me to get them there? Or was it all just coincidence?

After all, Jacob had known. He had told me what would happen just seconds after meeting them at the store. I couldn't shake his cold beaded eyes that pierced me as he prophesized their doom. It was something else not of his flesh and mind that looked at me.

Suddenly, I was delirious and, once again, wild questions swarmed my mind.

Was it possible for each of our demons to have been conspiring together while inside each of us? Or were they many (a legion of some kind) of the same dangerous conscious split between ours?

I had to shake myself; bring myself back to normalcy the best that I could. I was deep in my trip now, and I had never had such an intense mental breakdown such as this. My mind was squeezing itself. I was ranting silently of demons hiding within us, and I knew that this was absurd, but the drug was just too strong to convince it otherwise.

I had to stop before I babbled myself into an eternal state of delirium. The hellish screaming inside my mind made this difficult. It was like a distant calling echoing through a wide canyon.

The news of the murders had incidentally struck a sensitive nerve of paranoia in Helen and Lena. Both of their minds were beginning to drift carelessly into a spiraling descent of panic and chaos. They seemed as if they needed to cry, but the drug wouldn't allow it, so they were in a limbo state of emotional confusion. In this wretched gear, their minds would begin to turn on them in calculated nightmarish ways. And with the demon mastering the controls the effects could be incomprehensible. The only option available for them was to bite down, hold on tight, and wait for the ride to end. Regardless, the ticket had already been torn.

The news didn't seem to bother Hess. In fact, he seemed as distant as Jacob had. He had retired from trying to spot Jacob hiding in the night and had taken a seat beside me across the fire from Lena and Helen. His back faced them as he gazed upon the calmness of the water paradoxical from the tension behind him. Strangely, somehow, I knew that there was something teething on his soul. Perhaps it was his unfamiliar stare that hinted it. Or maybe it was just that whatever it was, was within us all and suggested only glimpses of what we thought we knew. I felt that it was the same force strangling me from within, only with him, it was exploding.

His trip was different.

Again, I was subconsciously rendering myself mad with psychotic nonsense. There was no demon. I had to remember to remind myself of this no matter how vociferous its bold cries became.

Lena was saying something like, "I can't believe I 've been in a house where people were actually murdered. That's just creepy."

Helen finished what Lena was conveying by saying, "It could've been any of us." Her voice was shaking as if she were running out of breath and her eyes were jaded.

"But it wasn't," I said trying to diffuse the impending fear I sensed deepening. "We're all right here."

"But we're not all here. Jacob is out there somewhere lost. Remember?" Lena pointed out at the forest rather dramatically.

Helen jumped to her feet suddenly and exasperated, "Oh God! What was that!" She was looking into the darker reaches of our surrounding; her mind was undoubtedly churning. Her performance had spooked me significantly and made me flinch awkwardly. Surprised, I asked, "what was what?" I could see that she was becoming frantic, uncontrollable even.

"That fucking noise! What was it?"

I looked to Lena to see if she heard anything, but her expression was as bemused as mine. She shrugged her shoulders and shook her head as she stood up slowly, not quite knowing what to do.

So, it had begun, I thought, just as I had feared all along. The cursed stuff that had lit our shadows like a beacon for the other side had allowed not only the gates of sanity to be breached, but be torn down.

We were all, indeed, mere beasts roaming in a desolate wilderness now, hunted by the dark bastard hiding inside us. I glanced at Hess. He was still as a statue, his face locked in rage. But silent all the while.

Helen had begun pacing in a small circle mumbling irately. Lena quickly put her arms around her, cooing her warmly.

"I can't do this! I need it to stop!" Helen ranted emphatically.

"Helen, it's okay," Lena said as she rubbed her on the back of her neck. "There's nothing out there. No one else heard anything." She attempted to be as soothing as possible, but I could hear in her strained tone that she was on the desperate edge and getting close to slipping. She continued, "Come and sit down with me, let's talk about something else. It's okay, really."

It was obvious to me that it wasn't going to be okay. The monstrous red dragon's eye was upon me, and Azzore had forsaken us. Hell may as well have been melting us in its fiery abyss. I glanced at Hess for some sort of sign that he would intervene, but he still only stared feebly into a menacing calm, oblivious to what was happening, which was unfortunate because her breakdown had left me on a sort of fringe that was dangerous to teeter.

Before I had an opportunity to say or do anything, she broke free from Lena's arms and combed through the night suspiciously with her phrenetic eyes.

"There it was again! What is that? What the fuck is that?"

I tried to suppress her illusions by saying, "It's just your mind playing tricks on you. Get a hold of yourself, for Christ's sake."

"No, I heard something. Don't fucking tell me that I didn't goddammit! I heard something moving right over there!" She was pointing decisively to a spot at the far corner of the woods where the pond met it on our side. She was shaking like some junkie two days in a withdrawal. Her voice was cracking away in between every syllable she mustered. She truly believed that there was something unseen stalking around us, and it was controlling her.

I suppose that she could've really heard something. Quite feasibly, it might've been a limb breaking from a tree or some small creature scurrying about in the fallen leaves, and it was just that her un-parallel perception was sprinting away from her. It was, of course, that imperious prowler distorting what was real and imagined, manifesting them as the same. I found myself reverting to the last time she had falsely perceived reality, suffering that furious psychedelic episode that could've easily ended badly, especially for Fifi. I wondered, as I watched her unfold from reality in the firelight, just how far she could take this nightmare.

I had a fiendish hunch that the demon had no boundaries for her. It would take her delusions and twist them into a mangled, bloody reality we would all have to suffer.

She shook but couldn't lose the fear. "I'm telling you, there's something out there," she exclaimed. Her tone was peaking at a broader height than before as the dread which often accompanied lucid hallucinogenic meltdowns strengthened. She began shaking her head frantically, murmuring incoherently and covered her face with her jittery hands. She acted as if she wanted to continue pacing, but for some reason couldn't, so she abruptly sat down in the grass. The fire exalted the night from her pale skin. The black make-up beginning to smear around her eyes seemed guilefully darker in the setting.

She continued, "I want to leave."

Lena appeared to have almost said something, but Hess intervened brutishly. His nostrils flared and his eyes seethed like some diabolical puppet. He had turned around, facing the fire, and the glow was sucked away by his enlarged pupils. He spoke harshly, yet eerily composed as if he were giving an order at a drive-thru. "Shut the fuck up, you stupid whore. There's nothing in the woods." He didn't smile or frown. He wasn't loud or quiet; he was like the Mona Lisa incarnated.

“Holy shit,” I thought quietly. I had to try hard to convince myself that what I saw and heard was real and not imagined. I had seen Hess angry, but always after provocation. Never had I seen him portray such unsolicited hostility towards anyone, even Helen. I found that I was at a complete loss for words and had zero solutions for anything that had transpired in the previous two minutes.

Hess, though, did seem to have the formula for the solution, at least in his own mind. Presumably, to snap her out and away from the fearful grip of her altered perception, his reasonable approach was to savagely berate her while monotonously using stern syllables. I couldn't comprehend how this supposed remedy could work; yet, I wasn't hip in the least as to what approach might drive away the hysteria meandering inside her mind.

I was occupied marshaling plots to help somehow when I heard her sheepishly quiver in fear. I looked up, across the fire, and saw that Hess had grabbed her by the shoulders and was shaking her rather tumultuously.

He shouted intensely, "You're freaking everybody out! Just shut the fuck up!" His face was at level with hers, and their eyes were at war with each other – hers were timid and breakable, on the verge of retracting to some distant hideaway, while his were intimidating and poised to strike.

It seemed that all I could do was observe what was unfolding. A part of me was actually thriving on the performance. Although I sensed a foreboding resolution, my curiosity was inflamed. I had no way of knowing if this was my own mortal flesh wanting more or the will of the one from the shadow. I had tried convincing myself that this prodding feeling was my own paranoia born from the drug enabling me, but now it was clear – I could never rid myself of the incredible feeling it was there; therefore it was.

As Hess held and shook Helen, Lena sprang to her defense. She shoved him away from her shouting, "Get away from her! Are you fucking crazy?" She snarled vehemently in his face with an incensed demeanor that was thick and palpable.

Brushing his hair from his eyes, Hess snapped back, "Fuck her! She's always doing something like this. For once I'd like to enjoy myself without her freaking out like some dumb whore!"

"You're the one freaking out," she rebutted as she stood face to face with him.

Helen was behind them sitting down. The features of her body were lightly traced by the flare of the fire. Her eyes were wide with fright as she timorously scanned the darkness in the direction of the woods. As if trying to expel the unwanted, filmy remnants of a nightmare, she shook her head flightily and covered her ears with her hands.

Through the dancing flames across from me, Hess and Lena were still squared off at each other. The anger that he displayed was unlike anything that I had ever witnessed. His entire body was rigid like that of a cat's ready and eager to attack its prey. There was a slight push from something within me, perhaps my own conscious, that instructed me to at least attempt to stop the madness before it spread and consumed us all; but also, I could feel the warm, enticing breath of the demon filling my soul as it chuckled, bidding me to do nothing.

Somehow, my mortal coil prevailed, and I forced myself up to help end this brewing catastrophe. He had his back to me, posed intimidatingly in a striking stance. Facing me as I approached was Lena, and I could see her cold, calculating gaze. I grabbed his arm to distract him and said, "Hey, it's cool man. Come sit with me and let's just chill." I paused, waiting for him to respond or acknowledge my presence.

There was a long silence as they continued to stare each other down, even the frogs stopped croaking from their places of hiding. Finally, just as I was about to say something else, Hess turned around slowly to face me. He was breathing heavily, and his enlarged, black pupils seemed copper-stained from the fire, making me think of the dragon wanting to consume me.

I shivered.

His mouth hardly seemed to move, but the coarse intent was unmistakable, as the words slipped through his lips softly, "Stay out of this."

Looking in his hollow, shark-like, eyes, I met his demon. It had consumed him and made a home. Hess was no longer the person who he had woke up as that day.

"Okay man," I said, fumbling the syllables. "Just don't hurt anybody. How could I ever explain anything plausibly?"

"Just go sit down and shut the fuck up," he said with an air of stringency.

Lena interrupted and said sensibly, "Why don't we all just sit down, okay? I mean, I've never been this messed up before. I'm really not sure what's happening." Tears were welling in her eyes. I could see her heart had just been broken.

For almost a full minute, the atmosphere had reversed, somewhat. Hess' demeanor had seemed to loosen, and it was as if he were contemplating her request. Perhaps his own mortal being was struggling to free itself as well. The silence didn't seem so dreary, as it had just moments before, but behind them, Helen, who had been huddled in her uneasiness and afraid of her own mind, sprang to her feet with fear and clinching her expression.

"Listen," she whimpered as she stared into the night again, lost completely once more.

Silence again washed us over as everyone listened.

"There it is again," she nearly moaned.

Sweating Mary, I thought. She was right. I heard it too.

.....

There was something coming from the woods behind me, moving intentionally slow as it shuffled through the brittle leaves that laid dead on the ground. It was precise, stopping and starting in short repetitive intervals. From where we gathered in the clearing, centered amongst the encompassing trees, it sounded as if the leaves were being raked over and over gratuitously slow.

"What the hell is that?" Lena asked. She backed away timidly from the noise. Hess took Helen's hand as they both stared into the black curtain of night.

Convinced now of her sanity Helen said, "You see, I'm not crazy! You all hear that. You see!" She was looking at Hess. He only stared in the other direction from her, focusing on the noise.

More so than at any other time that night, I was completely confused. I knew that it was mostly because the acid was barbarically raping my perception, and making me somewhat delusional, that I felt scared. Common sense should've warned me, it would seem, that it was merely an animal messing around, perhaps even two squirrels humping in the leaves. Yet I couldn't shake that I was somehow cognizant to the presence of the demon, exterior from myself now, caused by a mental manifestation into a physical state through my subconscious and that it was watching while lurking like some blood-craving predator.

Listening carefully, Lena stepped closer to the sound. "It's coming from over there now," she said pointing to the left of us.

I listened and like clockwork, the sound emerged again from the nothing into which we stared. We first heard it behind us on the west side of the pond off in the woods, but as Lena confirmed, it was now coming from our left near the south end, echoing through the trees in dramatically slow intervals.

The mystery of it all was enough to propel Helen into a kind of craze only comparable to how one would be expected to act after misfortunately witnessing an accidental beheading or some other gruesome incident. She began to clamor her words boisterously, "I wanna leave right now! There is something out there! Please, can we just go?"

Lena began to nod spastically. "Yeah. I wanna go too. This is too much." She turned around and began to walk towards Hess' car with Helen trailing closely behind her.

They had only made it a few steps when Hess called out, "Hey!"

His shouting pulled me from a lost gaze. The noise coming from the woods had lulled me into an uncomfortable paranoia.

"What is it?" Lena asked him. Her stare was impatient.

Hess disagreed defiantly, "We're not going anywhere."

"And why not?" Lena demanded to know. The raw hate returned to her stare as if a switch had been flipped.

"Because it's a fucking animal. Probably a squirrel."

"That's not a squirrel. Are you kidding?"

"How do you know it's not?"

"How do you know that it is?"

"Well, just what do you suppose it is then?" He asked peevishly.

Lena pursed her lips, and her eyes narrowed. Her voice seemed calm. "I don't know, Hess. But I'm really freaked out and so is Helen. I don't like it out here anymore."

Hess stared at her as he chose his words, "Even if I wanted to leave, I wouldn't. Are you forgetting that Jacob is still out there? We can't leave without him." I knew that he wasn't at all concerned about Jacob; he only wanted to disagree.

Helen pointed at me and said, "He can stay here and wait for him while you take us home."

"I'm not leaving him alone. Just chill out. Both of you." He cut his eyes at Lena as he said the latter.

I saw my chance at halting this potential nightmare and took it by saying, "No, it's okay man. I'll be good here. Thanks anyway, but you guys should get the hell out of here."

I had a strong hunch that I was due for a very long and dreadful night if the three of them didn't leave soon. For them, whatever they decided to do a hellish path awaited. Of this I was certain. At least if they left, then I wouldn't have to suffer their torment as the demon chewed their minds to pieces. For this reason, I desperately needed them to leave. Their hostile commotion was feeding my demon, making it stronger. There was no way of knowing how much time I had before I became like them.

Hess never looked at me, only kept his stubborn and angry stare on them. "I'm not going anywhere and neither are they. It's an animal; stop being a couple of pussies."

It was still problematic to ascertain what I was witnessing. He truly had become a different person entirely, not resembling the person I had known for so many years. As he posed in the night amid the soft glow of the fire, his feral countenance made him appear to be some fanged monster taunting all of us.

And like the breath of a foul god, the noise continued to stain the air.

Lena and Helen both appeared exhausted and pale; even in the glowing night their faces still seemed like luminous ghosts in the moonlight. Neither of them felt like arguing, instead seemed to be content with faking contentment with staying. They walked back to the fire, passing Hess as he rummaged through the pile of wood to feed the flames and sat down together becoming somewhat soothed by the warmth.

As much as I wanted all of them just to go, I needed to find real contentment with the fact that they weren't. I was clearly sliding on the razor-thin edge of a cognizant collapse, and I couldn't allow exterior variables to affect my condition. Although this was getting rather ridiculous, I could hear, and clearly discern, a separate but still entwined voice from my own screaming violently in the inner-most-confinement of my mind. I had to blindly assume that it was breaking free, or worse, already had.

The girls sat quietly, neither of them ever retracted their gazes from the flames. Fading embers sifted weightlessly like dust shedding from a star in front of their faces but their eyes, or minds, weren't interested in the beauty of it all. Instead, deep, powerful, perceptual malevolence skewered their thoughts. I know this because the same was happening to me. We each shared the same familiar decapitated stare.

The noise stopped. A sigh of relief escaped me, but it still wasn't enough to calm my raging mind. The wind had picked up a bit and slapped at the flames and swam freely through the few remaining leaves in the trees. Hess lurked around us after adding more sticks to the fire; his eyes and attention were fully fixed on the darkness beyond us.

It seemed that we were each in our own hell. In the deafening and horrible silence, my mind spewed fantastical thoughts, but mostly they just kept reverting to the vision I had in the stranger's yard. It was all so vivid in my mind again that I could feel the brightness of the earth vomiting the many beautiful and unknown colors after the screaming face fell from the stars. I thought of the heat from the dragon's breath melting me as it sniffed my presence in the dreamscape I had found myself in. I saw, with extraordinary recollection, the witch-goddess' beautiful Asian-like features devolve into some decrepit crone and taste from the cups of blood, using it to alter existence.

Most of all, I remembered the fear.

It was in the waning dusk of my reflections that I began to understand. I was finally able to consciously subject the pieces all in an orderly alignment so that they made sense, somewhat. I realized, through my enhanced meditation, that once I breached the threshold of my shadow an intense journey was unleashed upon my mind for me to take which served as an omen that I was meant to heed but failed to. I tasted the alien flavors of masochism shared by those beyond the shadow and was spared by their indulgences.

The questions remained, from what entity or deity or other-worldly being did the vision come from and just what in the hell did it all mean?

Something urged me to maintain mentally that it didn't matter now. It was far too late, I feared. The blaze had started already and I, along with my friends, had already begun to burn.

CHAPTER 16

The Beginning of the End

Fear can incite strange madness, and the unknown is a sure way to invite it. I know now that Hess was afraid. He was afraid just as Helen, Lena, and even I had been. The difference was, with him, his fear had been cockled to a state of deranged paranoia, resulting in anger and inevitably madness. It was the mysterious sound emerging from the darkness and swimming in the woods that dulled the edges of his sanity. At the time, all I could do was observe and ponder for I didn't know then what I know now.

If only I had.

It all started with the return of that goddamned sound. It rose from the depth of blackness suddenly and loud, snatching me from the sedation of my inner chaos. As I sat there, bathing in the warmth flowing from the fire and barely relating to reality at all, the noise escaping the woods seeped into my head, toying with my senses and becoming severely amplified. The overwhelming crackle of the dead leaves breaking and the echo of the slow brushes across the ground blotted out the cries from the fervid, red coals splitting at the base of the fire. I couldn't hear the frogs or the chirping songs from the crickets and grasshoppers. In my fragile state of mind, the sound had become the proverbial nails on a chalkboard, or a fat woman trying to get comfortable on a plastic hotel bed.

Futilely, I tried to negate its presence by shutting my eyes. In the short intervals between the sound, my heart lobbed in the pit of my stomach like a forlorn cork in the deepest sea. It did no good to shut my ears because the sound burrowed in my skin each time it rose.

Helen unexpectedly cried out again, and I was forced back into the perceived reality I had been part of. When I opened my eyes, I saw that Lena was already holding her and whispering calmness in her ears. I wondered how long this had been going on. It seemed and felt as if possibly Helen had been manic for some time before I ever heard her cry out. It was only a short time that passed, but she quickly became uncontrollable, despite Lena's best efforts to comfort her. The sound had given her a jolt of bad psychosis, and she was filled with it. She was sobbing, "no," and curling back away from the direction of the sound. She had been trying hard to stand and then finally broke free from Lena's hold and turned to face the direction spilling the sound. She turned back to face us, her eyes were terrified, and she said, "It's circling us. Just listen."

I was lost somewhere between reality and hell; stuck, still, somewhere in the shadow. Nothing in the environment I found myself in was familiar. It was as if the witch from my vision had come discretely in the confusion and reciprocated everything to align with madness symmetrically. Above us I saw the moon fill with blood and rain down in ember-like showers, giving the night a glow of some crass inferno. It clothed the ground making a filthy muck that reeked of death and disease. The wind screamed with peculiar laughs, mingling with the mysterious chimes haunting the air over the pond.

My mind had slipped down a dark tunnel, manifesting a false perception that symbolically caricatured reality. I closed my eyes and tried to focus more intensely. Although reality wasn't where I wanted to be at the moment, it was better than the nightmarish void in my mind.

I opened my eyes and saw Hess standing over Helen as she cried. His fists and jaws were clenched and an eagerness for destruction washed his eyes. I recognized the urgency to react but was still lost in my delusion and couldn't find any way to distract the fear and paranoia quickly conquering everything. Tears welled in her tired eyes and dripped off the end of her nose. She sobbed as terror stole away her breath. "Something is watching us," she said as she wept and looked up only to see him returning her gaze.

The hidden insects were laughing hysterically from somewhere in the night. The clouds were descending giant arms with talon-like fingers to rake the treetops and plow the blood-soaked soil. I tried to block the confusion and listened. I managed to shut my mind from the apocalyptic distraction and focus just on the noise. She was right. It was coming from the north end of the pond now, and so it did seem to be circling us.

As if this revelation was some sort of cure, all the hellish events occurring around me ceased. It was like the sun had come out in full radiance during the climax of a storm and chased away the beating rain and rolling thunder. The intense hallucinogenic terror faded, but it was still dark out, and the madness continued to reign unseen.

Immediately, I thought of Chris. I fantasized briefly that Lena had gotten the story wrong and that he wasn't dead in a bathtub with his wrists opened like the turned pages of a book, but rather slinking devilishly out there in the shadows. I saw him vividly in my mind, like a conscious nightmare, covered in crusted-over gobs of blood and gore, gnarling his teeth in a demented grin as the flesh hung loosely like tiny snakes from his wild hair and bushy beard.

Then, in another grotesque vision, I saw Jacob in the woods with his throat cut, face down in the thick mud of his own blood pouring from the slit. His clothes were torn and stripped like petty rags, and an unsympathetic blade had mutilated his body. In the moonlight, his blood was a black sludge soaking into the soil for the roots to greedily guzzle.

My train of thought crashed when I heard more screaming substitute for the crying. Jacob's torn and bloodied corpse was wiped clean from my mind by the sound of Helen's terror. This time, though, the authenticity of fear in her pitch was more pronounced and thorough, as opposed to her fear from plain bewilderment. I squinted my dizzy eyes and looked across the fire, waiting for them to adjust properly to the night faintly glowing beyond it. My confusion quickly grew into something more like a goddamned panic.

Helen was screaming, "Leave me alone! Stop it!" But her pleas were choked away by Hess' hands as her words became nonsensical gurgles.

Maniacally, yet calculated and calm, he was saying, "Shut the fuck up."

As she tried desperately to suck for air, I thought to myself: What the fuck? I could hear him breathing loudly between his uncomfortable bellows of hateful slandering. Aside from choking her, I could hear in his voice that his mind had finally faltered. One part of me wanted to run away into the woods and get lost with Jacob, while the other thought to stop him somehow. Then there was the curious demon part of me inclined to watch her die.

Her head and hair flickered back and forth as he shook her neck. Slowly, she began to lie down on her side as her body became too weak to try and fight back any longer. Her eyes were closing inevitably. I couldn't move; I couldn't even speak. I had been caught off guard by the violent performance. I had imagined a dozen or more different ways how the marauding shadow spirit could cleverly cause any one of them to lose their shit entirely.

Disappearing to shake hands with the devil on the dark side of the moon had seemed possible; even speaking in his cursed tongue for hours upon hours until the shadow's power ebbed in the drowning sunlight did as well; or maybe, perhaps, just deciding to take a swim in the nice, warm fire would have sufficed rationality. These things had seemed possible at the time, for when a powerful hallucinogenic agent is at work on your senses anything is possible. I was somewhat mentally prepared to handle anything like that, in a drug-induced kind of sense, but by no means was I ready for this shit. The shock had overtaken and even paralyzed me, for fuck's sake.

"Shut the hell up. For once just shut the fuck up! There's nothing out there," Hess continued. His eyes were wild with hate and bore extreme madness now. He was poised over her like a conquering god and squeezing tighter on her throat. Her mouth was gaped open, fighting to capture one last breath.

I heard a yell, "What the fuck Hess?" It was Lena as she jumped on his back flailing her fists at his head and face.

He let go of Helen's throat. Color began to flood back into her face as it plopped to the ground and she took a long breath of air followed rapidly by several short deep ones. She laid there, sobbing in the dirt by the fire.

"Get the fuck off me!" Hess yelled as he spun in circles trying to throw her off his back like a rodeo bull. She managed to hang on by digging her nails into his neck and clutching. I saw glimpses of his grimace as he spun around redundantly, crying out in anguish from her claws. The wind carried his screams far into the wooded fortress beyond. He reached over his shoulder and with an opened hand found her hair. Clinching it tightly, he easily yanked her over his shoulder and let her crash hard into grass covering the hard dirt. She landed close to where Helen still gasped for air.

In a quick burst, I heard her breath leave her lungs when her body made a dull thud as it hit the ground. She went limp entirely, her arms and legs appeared flimsy and she laid still for some time with Hess hovered over panting heavily. She regained mobility, slowly, and like a sloth rolled onto her side holding her chest where she had crashed to the ground.

It was at this moment that I felt the stronghold of the demon in my mind loosen. It may have been the adrenaline pumping in my veins that overthrew its dark tyranny, or just that it was done with me.

I stood up shouting, "What the fuck, man? Jesus!" I was walking toward him, fear and adrenaline emboldening me. "You've gotta get a grip, man!" I had my hands up showing that I meant no harm, but somehow the conveyance was lost.

Nonchalantly, he stooped to the burn pile and rummaged through the many sticks. He picked a thick, knotted branch resembling a baseball bat, and pointed it at me.

"Whoa, I come in peace," I said stopping in my tracks.

"Stay back," he warned coldly. He then turned his back to me as if he knew that his baleful tone and furious eyes were enough to deter me.

I stopped within a few feet from him, fanning flames of hope that I could talk him out of whatever violence he pursued. I saw his knuckles stretching white from his grip on the stick held by his side. He stood over Lena and Helen as they tried pitifully to get to their feet and catch their breath.

My mind chased the right kind of words. I didn't know what to say to a homicidal person experiencing a bad trip, who also may have been transformed by some special kind of evil. "Dude why are you doing this?" I knew the answer, even if he didn't – I didn't know what else to say.

When Hess spoke, it was as if he were someone else. My heart slowed down in mid-beat; my skin pricked up in my neck and arms. I felt cold. His voice seemed deeper and ancient. It was a stiff tone that held the intention to inflict pain. "Because I tasted it, and I want more."

Bemused and afraid I asked, "Tasted what, Hess?"

He turned his head slightly to where I could only see the side of his face, still though, and I could observe the dark pupils in his eyes absorbing all the moon's frail light. "I've tasted the forbidden pits of darkness," he rasped in that foreign tone. He looked dead at me and by God's fuck-stick if his eyes didn't shrink to nearly nothing and disappear before me as I watched. As soon as they had vanished, they popped back out at me, more pronounced and rounded, and began glowing some phosphorous yellow tint. He smiled and revealed to me his giant goddamn fangs protruding over his bottom lip and scraping his skin above his chin.

"Just hold on, man," I pleaded. "Please, don't fucking eat me, okay. You're not making any . . . . "

Before I could finish, Helen scrambled clumsily to her feet, hunched like some decrepit crone who wanted to hobble away. She only limped a few pathetic steps before Hess kicked her backside knocking her back down. She fell on her stomach, sliding her face across the gritty dirt in front of the fire. She was crying uncontrollably, and in the light from the flames, I could see blood leaving the fresh scratches on her face and trickling from her nose.

I stumbled to her, my head stinging from confusion, and tried to help her up, but in her pain and stifling presence of fear she thought I was Hess coming to inflict more terror. She began jerking and screaming, flailing like a deranged Pentecostal. One of her fists caught me across the cheek and caused me to stumble. "Helen, it's me!" I shouted carefully approaching her again as she still tried to stand. My mind was fetching for reality, still in the haze of my trip, and her crazed performance touched me deeply.

She kicked me with surprisingly great power and I stumbled back, contemplating trying again. I could see the flood of blood fleeing from her nose and the dirt stuck to the scratches on her face. The force of impact her head took when hitting the ground had caused her to sway with a dizzy dance trying to stand.

I didn't know what to do. The reality was a dysfunctional mother of a fuck kicking me in the ass, and I just stood there, frozen, watching her struggle to stand.

Behind me, I could hear Hess laughing, presumably, at the fit Helen was suffering. Before I could get to her again, as she thrashed in a suffocating grip of hysteria, she fell. As she tried to catch herself, her hand splashed into a sizzling red bed of coals. Beneath the profound scream from her lungs, I could hear skin pop as the flames licked at her and the coals melted her palm, soaking inside. Her screaming left a disturbing ringing in my ears that roiled inside my head. I was petrified as I watched her flop and twitch in expressive agony like some child ridding itself of an unclean spirit.

"Shut her up," Hess commanded me. I stared at him dubiously for I didn't know or understand anything. I felt as though I had been thrust unwillingly in T.S. Elliot's *'The Wasteland'* where the purpose is reversed, and misery prevails.

Without thinking, following my own questionable instincts, I charged at him determined to finally end the madness. I thought that if I could only subdue him, then I could prevent any further reign of horror he might try. Surely then, this calamity would dissolve. Although, inevitably, our lives would never be the same, for how could any of us ever speak of this again?

I rushed at him with blind aggression; not thinking, only doing. Once I was within reach, I threw a wild right hand. If I had landed it, his septum would certainly have been shattered into minuscule fragments, and he would've been sucking blood and snot for the rest of the night. But as it happened, I missed. My fist flew over his head as he quickly ducked out of the way and my momentum shifted me slightly off balance.

For a moment, I felt as though I might fall like some dizzy child looking at the clouds while spinning in circles. In one terribly smooth, expertly maneuvered motion Hess swung the stick as he dodged me and hammered my knee with the knotted end. I screamed out in anguish and dropped to the ground as a sharp, penetrating pain gushed throughout my body, I gasped from the throbbing blood flow pulsating vigorously.

"I told you to stay back," he hissed rubbing his hand across his shaved head. He held the stick down by his side like a favored weapon from an ancient war. He paced leisurely, yet troublesome in his mannerism, mumbling incoherent pieces of sentences.

I was between Helen and Lena. Helen was by the fire, crying. The fire's glow could barely reach Lena, who was still curled in U-shape on the ground trying to find her breath. Hess was lingering in the night watching us all. His morbid stare was intensified by the violence playing out.

The pain swelled in me. Helen's pain came with an out-lash of wails that probed me, making my anguish worse. I began gnashing my teeth trying to ebb my pain, and through my squinted eyes I saw Hess walk calmly to her, mumbling something about a whore. She was oblivious to him at that moment as she shrieked by the fire only a few yards from me, holding her blistered hand.

"Hess! You motherfucker! Stop!" I shouted through my pain. The stick had snapped my knee out of place, and I could feel that it was distorted. I couldn't stand and I could barely speak.

She saw him coming and tried to crawl away into the enticing cover of the night, wailing a song of pain. She made it only a few yards before he forced his foot on the back of her neck, shoving her face into the grass as she screamed. Discordantly, her cries mingled with the pleasant buzzes and chirpings of the insects oblivious to the macabre.

"Where you going, bitch?" Hess asked rhetorically. His voice became the vestibule for the demon imbruting his personality. With a serene expression, he raised the stick over his head vertically as if he were going to stab it straight through her, but instead rammed the blunt end of it with flashing strength to the tender area just under her rib cage and above her kidney. A pitiful moan escaped her as she again searched for her breath and writhed there in the blades of grass like a puppy playing; only she wasn't playing.

Propelled by the pain stabbing in my knee and the helpless fear showering my senses I screamed, "No! You bastard! What are you doing?" I tried to stand but my leg crumbled beneath my weight. A crashing pain, even sharper than before, lashed me.

He ignored me and turned his attention to Lena, who was cautiously rising to her feet. She was holding her side and wincing, presumably pressurizing the area that absorbed most of the impact from her fall. He left Helen gasping for air face down in the grass and with nimble swiftness scurried to her, the stick clutched with both hands ready to strike. A smirk that needed satisfying spread across his face and his eyes gleamed ferociously. He was akin to some giddy maniac in a slasher film.

I screamed to warn her, for she had her back to him, but before I could the stick had already clapped the back of her head. The sound was nothing other than sickening. It was like the unmistakable crack of a home run hit ball. She fell instantly. A dark blotch of blood matted her hair as it leaked from a gash left by the impact. All the energy and light left her eyes as they rolled to the back of her lids, stowing themselves away from the horror.

I attempted to stand, unsure of anything anymore yet again. Words flew from my tongue without any thought, "You piece of shit!

What the fuck, man? I'll kill you! Do you hear me? I'll fucking kill you!"

A laughing that was not my own infested my mind. I could hear it far away in the recesses of my conscious. It was the same stranger that had been screaming to break free. I recognized the baleful tone. I was overcome by it. It seemed that my head would explode if it didn't quieten. I looked to the sky, and it opened like a thin veil. All the clouds and stars were pulled away by some unseen force and the emptiness that was the sky peeled away like a scab. There was some cosmic eye opened wide, bleeding a kind of putrid secretion, coloring the void where the sky had been in a deathly, sickish way.

I closed my eyes and tried to shut my mind from the terrible hallucination. The laughing began to fade, and the sound of the fire cracking collaborated with the dread of Helen gasping desperately for air.

"What was that," I heard Hess ask sarcastically. I looked up and found him standing over me, caressing the stick with his hands. "You're going to kill me?"

In the time frame of only a few seconds, several things occurred to me. One was that I didn't want to die by being beaten to death – being eaten alive had always been my worst fear of ways to die, but I had never considered being beaten until at the moment death finally arrived to take me away. Incidentally, it became number one. Another realization I had at that moment is that this was no hallucination, and very much real.

But the most prominent thing that stood out to me was a sound. It was the same sound that had been stirring around in the woods and had been the start of this terrible drama. The strangest part was that it was right behind me brushing coarsely through the grass. It started and stopped in the same short intervals as before and was inching closer.

Before I could turn to look, I saw the stick out of the corner of my eye approaching with bullet-like force and speed. And then a cold blackness sacked me as I went to sleep.

CHAPTER 17

A Macabre Awakening

When I opened my eyes, I was lying on my side and was instantly jarred by a throbbing pain originating in the temple region of my head just behind my eye. It spread like running water through the rest of my head. I felt the warm flow of blood trickling down the side of the face and the obtrusive swelling above my left eye. The earth around me was a blurry maze of light and shadows, flickering inconsistently as if from faulty wiring in the cosmos, hindering my ability to see. I shut my eyes and waited for the ringing in my head to dissipate and hoped that when I opened them the world would rest and be still.

For a brief time, I didn't remember where I was or what was happening. Though the ringing in my head continued to validate the pain, everything else began to shrink back into focus. I remembered the strange sound enchanting Helen into a frightened beast. I remembered how her fear had even latched onto me. Then, like a bullet ripping through my mind, I remembered what Hess had done. A part of me fantasized dubiously that I had imagined it all; that it was all just part of some psychedelic coercion. Only I sure as fuck knew I hadn't imagined it; the pain in my head and blood on my face attested the fact.

Suddenly, and powerfully, the fear cradled me in its skeleton arms again and refused to let me go. I felt the extreme urge to scream.

I opened my eyes, and they adjusted to the gothic image of a yellow moon brimming through thin transparent clouds. The fire's glow had faded substantially from before I had been knocked unconscious and wisps of smoke left the red coals, spreading out and over and through the trees. The fire faintly beamed like a discarded trinket.

I tried to sit up, but I was paralyzed by the blood bubbling in my head. I carefully lifted my head and propped myself on my arm, still lying on my side. Directly in front of me was the dying crackle of flames in the fire, they faintly pushed a breath of warmth that stroked my skin and helped clear my mind, even subsiding my raging senses. The ringing that had stifled all that was within me had faded away like morning mist on a clear lake. Although the stabbing pain bit at my knee as I moved, I was able to maneuver myself into a sitting position. I clutched my head between my hands and closed my eyes, feeling them beat against my skull.

I thought of Hess, how he bashed Helen, Lena, and myself with the stick. His mind was detuned badly, and there were no knobs to fix him. The terrible fact occurred to me that this trip was starting.

I had to find him, and hopefully, I wouldn't have to kill him in some dramatic way.

This was real, and I could feel the fear roiling around like the waters under a deep storm. There was no escaping the inevitable.

When my mind stabled itself from the heavy throbs of pain, I opened my eyes, but it was like falling asleep again and tossed into an inescapable nightmare. A visual and audible torrid of horror crashed through me like a prodigious wave. In my concussive and confused state after waking, I had mistaken wailing screams for the ringing in my ears. The screaming, that was not my own, nor from some entity within me, filled the air and choked away all other sounds.

There was some growling too – a voracious breath, it seemed, gobbling everything around me.

What was it?

I realized it was Lena calling out weakly, I recognized her distinct tone wallowing in the screams, but I couldn't see her for my eyes hadn't completely adjusted to the swirling mixture of darkness and weakening fire-light. As they slowly did settle, the darkness peeled away, and her screaming stopped, but I could still hear echoing whimpers and sobs only feet from me. A somber and beaten figure, who I knew instinctively to be Lena, crawled towards me. The closer she got, the withering flames revealed more of her in their light so that I could see. Her clothes were torn, and she was bleeding from somewhere because it covered her neck and arms, even down to her breasts. Her hair was matted in red tangled strands. The blood seemed to be everywhere. She crawled slowly, dragging her torso and legs through the dirt at the edge where the grass began. It seemed that each push she made forward hurt, as she grunted and groaned under her breath. She was inches from me, and her arms were shaking from holding her weight.

"Help," she whispered. Fear draped her bloodied complexion. Her arm was stretched out to me as her body laid still. Instinctively I reached out for her if only to comfort her with my touch. A powerful sting of pain shot through my knee and made me cry out as I reached. At that same moment, her arms failed, and she collapsed, missing my hand. Her face fell into the dirt and puffs of dust exploded into the air as she exhaustively exhaled her pain. I wanted to help her, to be the hero, but when I moved it was as if my knee was in the grip of some feral beast's teeth.

Pain is a bitter reminder, and it brought back a flood of terror. My mind, body, and soul recoiled. My heart was like a rusted piston frantically thrashing in my chest. I shook uncontrollably as if I were freezing; only I wasn't; I felt as if I were on fire inside and out.

Where was he? Maybe he went for a walk to clear his head, and we're safe from his fearful wrath.

Where in the hell are my cigarettes? I thought. I really wanted one. I felt that I might die if I didn't have one. I was too captivated by the pain to search for them, so I just suffered.

This was bad, I thought, and the goddamn fire was going out too.

I looked around me, but all I could see was growing darkness.

Where was Helen? Why was Lena the only one here, bloody and beaten?

Then, over Lena's gurgling sobs, I heard the sound. It was coming from where Lena had crawled from and was getting closer while staying true to its same ominous pattern.

Nearly whispering I called out, "Hello."

Lena lifted her face from the dirt, and the dying fire washed us with its weak glow. She could hardly mouth the words but said, "It's him." Then her voice cracked with desperation. "Help. You've gotta help me." Blood poured from her nose, spilling over chunks of dirt sticking to her scratched face. Her lips were puffy and split on the bottom. The blood had started to dry into a black scab dressed in dirt. Behind matted strands of hair, she conveyed every bit of her fear with a frigid stare. It drove itself through me like a stake and ravaged me like some horny creature. I can't say if there is a way to describe such panic.

The noise finally stopped, but Lena was still crying. Her breath would escape her completely between each grueling sob causing her to search tirelessly for another.

"Hess, this isn't cool man." I never expected a reply. I did, however, hope to hear some movement. The silence was more sinister and haunting than the noise. Silence has a way of sneaking beyond your thoughts and settling in the pit of your senses, twisting them into tight knots.

The coals hissed as the diminishing flames had now almost completely disappeared. The light dwindled but still managed to pierce the darkness slightly. At the barrier, where the faded glow met the waiting night, I saw I shadowy silhouette in the smoke of something, or someone, hunched in a lurking pose over Lena's outstretched body. I felt my heart harden like a stone and drop with a thud at its sight. As I tried to discern what I saw, the figure descended on her like a vulture on a carcass and began wantonly thrashing her body. She tried to defend herself by kicking and scratching at its dark, hidden face while screaming through the blood purging in her throat.

I still couldn't see it or what exactly it was, although, it appeared humanoid. Lena tried desperately to break free from its grasp by flapping her body and thrusting anyway that she could, but its head was cemented to her body, twitching as it shook as violently as she did. Over her screams, the sound of it grunting and moaning in furious pleasure came from the thing. A surge of wind gave breath to the flames, and they swelled for a moment. The glow was long enough for me to get a clear picture of what was happening. It was as if the goddamned thing was eating her alive (it was eating her alive!).

It was on top of her gnashing its teeth into her flesh and then ripping it away with jerking thrashes, much like a frenzied shark feeding. A red mist of blood from a severed artery in her thigh sprayed into the air and dissipated into the dying light of the fire. The more she fought and writhed to get away, the harder it slammed its fists into her chest and face, pounding them like a drum. The sound was unforgettable; the bones in her face were cracking under the smothering fist was like eggs shells breaking under a cloth. It was pinning her down with a forearm pressing on her throat and the weight of its body on her waist. Her screams weakened to shy throaty cries, choked by her own teeth and blood. The sound of the skin tearing away from the nerves and muscles underneath preyed upon my mind. Thick, dripping tentacles of flesh and tendons hung over the body wiggling spastically like worms having seizures. It spat away chunks of the detached flesh and chewed what remained in its mouth, all the while moaning with intense gratification.

All the while its face was hidden by the shadows.

Surely this was no human, but some shapeshifting fiend that stumbled upon us. Better yet, this was only a dream that I would awake from momentarily, just as I had in the stranger's yard. I wanted to believe this, but it was just all too real.

I found myself yelling for it to stop. My screams carried over Lena's, which were now merely shallow breaths suffocated by this evil night, for the flames were again dying. Her body, nor her mind, had the power left to resist the clutch of teeth tearing her apart. She laid still and finally quiet, perhaps from the shock of pain – or even death.

I could hear myself breathing heavily, panting like a happy dog. Only I wasn't happy. I was afraid of this unknown thing tearing Lena apart piece by piece with every bite. I held my breath in, to politely usher in peace within myself before dying, but it didn't work – my pounding heart forced the air from my lungs and stoked the fear. Somewhere between the bass of my heart thumping in my throat and the scrappy sound of breath shoved from my lungs, I plead with all my fear leading my words, "Please! For fuck's sake, man! Don't eat me!"

I had almost been eaten alive on more than one occasion, so this predicament ailing me didn't suffice my fortune in the least.

It stood straight up from the crouching position it was in over Lena's bloody body. Casually it raised its hand to its face and presumably wiped away the flesh and dripping blood from its mouth, for in the amber glow still fading gradually it appeared as a daunting shadow; a menacing black shape imbibing the darkness. Turning and facing the opposite direction of me it limped away. Its left leg seemed dead, dragging through muddied dirt, thickened by Lena's blood. The foot was rigid and sideways, dragging the ground in haunting intervals; raking the dirt as it walked – a limping shadow in the night.

I shuddered at the thought of it circling us in the woods the entire time, studying and stalking us like a trained predator.

It grabbed a stump from the wood pile and came back to the fire dragging behind it its lame foot. It tossed it, and I could almost hear the desperate flames rejoice in song as they ate upon the fresh offering.

As the flames grew stronger and the night slithered further away from me, the figure limped past me into the curtain of darkness dropping where the glow receded. It slipped, still disguised, into the darkness behind me.

I was still pinned by the pain in my knee and the dizziness in my head. I let out a useless cry as I tried to turn around. I sighed and grunted, 'Hess?"

There was no answer.

I front of me Lena's body caught my eye. Her clothes were torn away brutally, while pieces still clung to her body damp with blood. Gore slid off her stomach as pools of it formed where its teeth had sunk in and pulled chunks of her away. Her nose was broken and smashed askew to the right side of her face. Her eyes were swollen and shut like a pounded prize fighter's. Gaping, repulsive, wounds formed grids all over her, from her breasts down to her inner thighs just above her knees. From the overflowing pools of blood, small red creeks spilled down her skin.

I couldn't see all the love and tender-spirit in her face any longer as she lay listless under the moon. It was as if it all had been melted away by the fire, but the fact was that it had been swallowed by a monster.

The glow had spread further to my right, between myself and Lena's body. My mind recoiled at what my eyes captured. It was Helen lying on her back, with her clothes bloodied and drenched. Her throat was torn out, and thick black streams of blood had formed a gummy pool around her that seemed like oil in the fire-light. She lay lifeless with two broken sticks pushed through her eyes. They protruded upward into the night like some morbid religious monolith. Wisps of smoke curled out of her gouged sockets and spiraled around the sticks like a gray serpent – they were still burning in her skull. I perused her body further and noticed the vesicular wounds deforming her hand. They seemed as fresh as when she had first fallen into the fire.

"Great Son of Sam," I thought. "What kind of cannibal orgy had I awakened into? Did this type of stuff ever actually happen?"

I knew that I was in deep, deep shit here. I could only hope for this deranged beast to go away before it ate me too.

And if it didn't kill me, I could never explain this. Either way, I was fucked gloriously.

I heard the grass brushing behind me. It was moving again. I turned my head to the left, then to the right, trying to find the noise.

"Hess, come on man. What the hell." There was no reply. In fact, it stopped moving. But it was close; I could feel its presence lusting me. For some reason, I foolishly said, "come on man. We can fix this. It's nothing."

Silence.

I waited for what seemed like an eternity for some reply, or even just movement again, but nothing came. The wind eventually shifted, and the trees hummed together in harmony. The water from the pond rolled up onto the bank, petering back calmly. The flames changed directions, and their ardent flickering glow spilled over to the left of me. I felt the tranquil warmth they expelled, but what they showed me groped my insides and tugged.

Near me, just out of my reach lying on his side was Hess. All I could see was his backside, but that was enough to show me that he was dead. The back of his head was missing. His cranium was opened like a mouth and was vomiting chunks of brains and gore. Lying beside him was a large stone ornamented with pieces of blood-soaked hair and skull pasted to it.

I tried to steady my weight. The dizziness was returning. The earth began to spin as my head swam away to depths impossible to reach. I braced my hands on the ground to make it stop, clenching my eyes shut.

The acid was still running free. Apparently, having your knee snapped out of its socket and getting knocked unconscious doesn't slow it down. There were unrecognizable sounds marauding the night. Somewhere a drumming hum vibrated my ears. The chirping of insects became abnormally loud screeches in my head; it was as if each individual chirp was broken into a million separate waves of sound, darting through the air like missiles piercing my mind. I kept my eyes closed, for I could still feel the rumbling of the ground. My psyche had become a mess. I felt as though I might explode from the inside.

It was then that the exaggerated sounds fucking with me all stopped at once. The unusual silence beckoned my fear to swell. From behind me, breaking the quiet, I heard it begin to shuffle across the earth. With my eyes still closed I imagined the stiff, dead limb attached to the monster brushing through the grass. It was only inches away. I knew this because I could hear it breathing (at least I thought I could). I opened my eyes in time to see it pass me by and stand still between myself and the fire, moving like lost spirits in a dream, then slowly it turned around. The aroma of flesh sickened me. It pivoted its dead foot in the dirt as it turned to face me never lifting it off the ground.

It sat down directly in front of me, eyes burning like lava, reflecting the frenzied flames. The mystery of the noise from the woods was now revealed.

It was Jacob. His countenance now devilishly serene, as if he found some purpose and was eager to fulfill it. He stared at me with searching, marauding eyes gripping my soul. Calmly, he brushed his hair from his brow and picked a piece of skin from his teeth. With a sophisticated air and a pious tone, he smiled at me, spreading his blood-stained lips kindly and said, "hello Argos."

CHAPTER 18

The Sad Eyes That Blossomed Evil

It's difficult to imagine anything as foreboding as my friend Jacob as he stared at me with an evil lust and a blood-stained face. It is equally as impossible to fathom the clustering of darkness pervading his presence. Although the fire roared and crackled in the background and bred a hopeful glow, the night and all its stark qualities still, somehow, invaded all that was around him. It was as if his realm of existence summoned it all like some gravitational imbalance. The force of his presence conjured an array of peculiar feelings of receded uneasiness, along with emotions bundled and stuffed deep within me.

I can't recall him ever blinking, only that his eyes bore into me like a tunneling parasite, prying loose every nerve connecting me. His apathetic composure juxtaposed to the heavy breaths of the fire behind him forming light was like a forbidden portrait of madness and evil coming to life before me. It was mainly fear that roamed freely inside me.

Blood caked his face like a tattered mask. He eerily reminded of the clown from my mescaline journey. Only he wasn't. He was something else – something else entirely.

"Jacob," I whispered, but somehow, I instinctively knew that name wasn't relevant any longer.

As if confirming my intuition, he said grimly, "Do not pretend to assume that I am anyone that you know."

I choked on my fear at the sound of his defiant voice, unlike the Jacob I knew, and stared into his pregnant pupils. His face was pallid and sickly, like a desperate vampire thirsting in a desolate land.

I tried not to shake my words, but with a trembling voice I asked, "Who are you?"

"You will find out, seeing as you do not already know." He smiled nefariously. His teeth were still red with blood.

"What have you done? Why?"

"Do not worry yourself with questions you cannot understand yet – as much as you believe that you can." His smile didn't wane in the least. It was terrible and beautiful at the same time.

I had to seriously explore my senses and thoughts before realizing that this was real, even though every part of me wanted it not to be. I knew that I was tripping, that much was certain. I knew that I was among my mutilated peers and the smell of their blood enhanced by the heat was nauseating. I knew that my knee was seriously fucked up because the pain was poking fun at me. I knew that I was stuck where I sat.

What I didn't know was why Jacob was sitting before me looking like some demon with a full belly.

Also, just why in Poseidon's swimsuit did he call me Argos?

"Why didn't you call me by my name? Surely you know it." I asked.

He spoke behind that same cunning, forged smile saying, "That name is far more fitting for you. I chose it specifically for you because you are no longer who you used to be. You compete for attention that you do not deserve and seek petty approval that you do not need. Just as you sit there now, unable to move, rotting in your pain. Also, you were the first to recognize me. So, your new name fits."

It was strange and horrifying hearing Jacob speak so casually and demeaning. His voice had taken on the resemblance of a mad genius speaking in wild tongues of poetry.

"I don't understand," I said dumbly.

He nodded and with mock-sympathy responded, "I know. I did not expect that you would. Your kind rarely understands anything unless it is hand fed and shoved down your throats neatly."

It seemed as if I were trapped in a dream and was aware that I was dreaming. Everything I knew to be senseless and unfamiliar somehow seemed logical and normal, although, I had no idea what was, and what was what. It was Jacob's form that I was seeing, but I knew that it wasn't him. Everything that made him was absent in that stare. Even his quirky mannerisms and shy demeanor had been replaced. Now he appeared dignified and confident. The way that he glowered over me as if I were his toy to misuse and discard made him seem like a rebellious god.

"What do you want?" I asked.

He tilted his head back gently and laughed sarcastically to the sky. The flames, as if emboldened by his mirth, grew behind him and gave the appearance of a gleaming crown of dancing fire upon his head.

When he looked back at me his lips glistened with the blood of my peers, and he said calmly, "I only want to exist in your world. I must exist."

Probing, I asked, "You're not of this world?"

His response was cryptic at best. "Well no, and yes."

It was odd having a conversation with the person that just mutilated and ate my friends, but I felt some pull harnessing me into the intense dialogue. Perhaps it was a thirst for knowledge; or just my survival instinct taking over and forcing the conversation on, for the longer he spoke, the longer I lived.

I should've known I was playing into its hands.

"What does that even mean?" I asked. "Either you are, or you're not."

He looked at me, grinning widely, and shook his finger at me. "I like you Argos. I really do. That is why I chose to speak to you. I do love to conversate. I rarely get the opportunity to do so."

He paused and dropped his eyes to my leg. His grin faded, and in all seriousness, he said, "I am sorry about your knee, by the way, but you certainly would have thwarted my intention if I had not …, well, you know." He nodded at my knee laying crooked in the dirt.

I focused on what he was saying for moment, then declared, "But that was Hess who hit me; not you. I remember."

"Yes, yes. And no," he replied scooting closer to me, close enough now to where I could see clearly the soggy pieces of flesh stuck to his cheeks. "As I was saying, I like you Argos. I want to explain what I can, if I can, in a way that you can understand. More often than not, mortal minds can be too adjusted to their own world to understand some things."

When he finished speaking, my heart had slowed to a steady rhythm and I became relaxed in an abnormal kind of way. Even the flames seemed to shrink away and fall listless to his voice. I could sense fear nipping at my heels, but incidentally, his calm presence and soft tone cast a certain serenity intoxicating me like a powerful pheromone.

Curiously I asked, "Explain what?" I had forgotten all about dying as calmness swept over me like a warm cloud and every part of me, even to this day, felt that his presence succumbed me.

He studied me, pretended to muse my question, and then answered methodically, "I will tell you everything you want to know. All you have to do is ask. Is that fair?"

"Okay," I answered, already knowing what I wanted to ask, "What are you? Who are you? I mean, you aren't Jacob. Are you?"

There was hardly a pause, and his intrepid voice expanded in the night like a lion's purr in a dark cave, "I am evil." The fire breathed behind him – with him.

Unsatisfied by this obscure explanation, I pushed for an answer I could be comfortable with, "That's not what I meant. Who are you?"

As fear ruptured in me like a festering infection, he plainly stated with the mien of a deity, "As I said, I am evil. Nothing more or nothing less. I have no name. No identity. Your mortal vocabulary only defines me. I am too pure and absolute to be named. This is what and who I am."

I quibbled indirectly, "I don't understand."

"Sure, you do. You just have not realized it. Not yet anyway." Certainty reigned unscathed in its expression. It was an observation that chilled me to the core of my mortality.

"You referred to me as a mortal," I said still trying to scratch at the surface, "I assume that you aren't."

It answered, "I told you, I am evil. Do you consider evil to be mortal?"

I weighed my response quickly and responded, "I suppose that a mortal can be evil."

As if it expected such a mundane reply it answered, "In your worldly perception of truth this is accurate – but it is not. A mortal possessing evil is just that – a mortal who possesses evil. As I said, I am evil, yet I am no mortal. If your friend Jacob could speak right now, he would tell you that I am completely in control, not him."

It may as well have been speaking a dead language. I was certain it said what I should have understood, or at the very least grasped, if even loosely, some sense of comprehension, but I didn't. If there was any meaning in its baffling riddles, I was oblivious.

It must have read my blank expression loosening to a dumb stare because it said, "I am only allowing you so much time to understand. Whatever you should ask, you should ask."

There was an optimistic part of me that wondered if this was some cruel game that everyone was playing on me. I found myself hoping that at any moment my friends would spring up jovially, chuck hysterically, and shout "gotcha." But as my eyes trained on their bodies becoming more rigid by the fire, I recognized that this was no joke and that the fallacious hope that I fathomed was instead a level of my own madness.

My next question came to me without much thought or emphasis. I blurted it almost as if I were speaking to myself. "So, you are immortal then? Like a god?"

"Oh, Argos," it replied smiling, "you do flatter me, even if you do not wish to." Its trapping smile melted away my nerves and made me feel naked. "But you still do not understand. I am just evil — neither mortal or immortal. I am. I exist, always, but I am not alive or dead."

"That doesn't make any sense," I argued. I felt myself being cleverly drawn into an infinite conversation that would only chip away what little of my sanity I had left, leaving me as nothing more than a lunatic choking on the shadows of its mind. "I am speaking with you. You are speaking. You exist because you're alive."

It clapped its hands, and the sound reverberated in the dark woods eerily as it laughed. "Now this is most certainly why I wanted to talk with you, Argos. You know everything but understand nothing. I do love that. It is my favorite flaw." It grinned contortedly, narrowing Jacob's deep black eyes, sinking them in his stained, yet pale, face. It had a forcible demonic stare that pinched at my skin as its eyes perused me. "Tell me, then, what do you know of mortal beings opposed to a god?"

The question turned over in my mind several times, and finally, I said, "I can't possibly know everything, but I can tell you what I believe based on what I've experienced and how I've been taught."

"Very well," it cooed. "that is indeed why you possess a mind."

Oddly becoming even more comfortable in my pain and in its presence, I slid myself even closer. I could hear it breathing and smelled the decay of hot flesh escaping its mouth again. I felt the fire rise, seeming to obey its temper, as it became enthralled by my eagerness to play its game. I cleared my throat and calmly began, "mortals are limited to everything: life, love, happiness, pain, even memories. We exist only to die and use up what we can of the world we're limited to, while we wait to leave it."

It continued to gaze at me with interest, although I felt that it already knew what I was going to say before I said it. Nonetheless, I was propelled to continue and finished, "A god, on the other hand, is unlimited to all of this and so much more, yet needs none of it, which would contradict most beliefs that a god demands to be worshipped and loved – or praised. Why would an all-powerful being, unlimited to everything, demand such a thing that mortals crave? Kings and false prophets demand to be worshipped and praised by their inferior subjects because they are mortal and are chained to their desires, thus constantly feeding them to replenish them. A god, however, shouldn't need such petty approval from lesser beings or even care. Worshipping and praising are mortal fabrications contrived through what they deem to be necessary from a well-disciplined primitive conscious."

Those strange, abysmal eyes picked me apart and from the collected composure radiating outward, I felt assured that it was becoming more comfortable in Jacob's body and mind. I wondered, as it stared at me blankly, if it had completely consumed his soul as well as his mind; perhaps both in the same ferocious bite.

Finally, after a long and dreadful collection of seconds, it frowned for the first time and said, "You have a very morose view of your existence. Your prognosis would suggest a mortal fabrication in order to gain a certain amount of control. Which would suggest that I had a part to play." It lit a cigarette and seemed to embellish the taste. I wondered foolishly if it was Jacob enjoying it, or the evil. It kindly offered me one, and I took it. It then reached over and lit it with Jacob's lighter.

"Despite being evil, you're very polite," I inquisitively noted.

"I am only trying to make you feel comfortable. I hope that it is working."

I glanced at my murdered and mutilated friends rotting hastily in the heat and a sick, dizzying feeling flooded my insides. "Not entirely," I mustered to say.

It noted my attention distracted by their bloody corpses and tried to appease me. It smiled and soothed, "I am sorry Argos. But I am evil. I exist to oppose good. That is disquieting to most of your kind. I am, truly, everything that you deem terrible and appalling. Just as you say that you exist to die and reap your limitations in the meantime, I exist to dwell and prosper in the darkest places of your mind, showing myself only to feed. I adjust my tactics to stimulate my needs, according to the mind of course."

It stopped short before finishing and collected its thoughts briefly, "I am getting carried away and ahead of our conversation; please excuse me. I would like very much to go on with our discussion while there is time. It does serve a purpose for your understanding, but for that to happen I acknowledge that you must be comfortable." It darted its eyes to Lena's body, then swam them to Helen and then Hess. "Would it help if I hid them? Perhaps in the darkness behind you where you cannot see them?"

"No," I insisted, "that doesn't change the fact that they are dead."

"But is that not what you humans are apt to do: hide truths as to pretend that they do not exist? I must confess, myself, that I have construed quite decisively that I have flourished lushly because of this unanimous trait since the very beginning of your existence."

I had fallen, once again, under its spell. I was unshaken and enthralled by its engaging dialogue. I found that I was only concerned with what it had to share with me. My friends, whom I had loved greatly, lying scattered around me and beginning to stink of death, were suddenly of no consequence to my feelings. Its presence seemed to draw all my curiosity to the surface and negate every other thing around me but itself. Its power was true of some other place that I had to know more about.

So without fear or hesitation, only instinct and a blind quest for answers, I began to search its knowledge more precisely.

"If you're neither mortal or immortal, then where do you come from?" I asked genuinely with my eyes solely connected with it.

It lowered its head in a polite kind of bow, laughing gently, and applauded me. "Ah, alas, I see that you have slain your apprehension and still seek the truth. This is what I had hoped. I believe that I understand what you are inquiring; you want to know why I exist. Correct?"

I nodded.

"Very well," it began to speak again dancing the words right off its tongue, "Ever since your kind came into existence, I have existed. You see, the most common belief that you humans share is that your creator is omnipotent and wholly good. This is more of a necessary need, or excuse, implemented subconsciously by the mortal mind to take comfort with insecurities, and to justify their own weaknesses. But this belief cannot be so if I am here conversing with you. I am evil. Do you understand?"

I shook my head, slowly, and answered honestly, "Somewhat. I suppose."

It rolled its eyes teasingly, picking up a small pebble from the ground and tossing it at me, striking me lightly on the chest. "Argos, use your mind. That is why you have it. You see, saying that God is wholly good and knowing that He created all things suggests that I cannot exist. For how can I, then? Am I not the physical manifestation of your fears?"

I frivolously asked, "Well that is the question worth answering, isn't it?"

"Indeed. If you would like, I can hint to you that He did create everything and everything He created contains a bit of all of Him. Everything. Even me."

It paused and waited as if already knowing that I would object.

I chose my words carefully. Remembering its every word from before. "You said that you had existed ever since we have. Doesn't that suggest that you were spawned by us because we have the ability to think for ourselves? It doesn't entirely imply that He created you. Only that He allows you to exist in respect to free-will."

"Oh, but it does imply just that. Without you, I would not have a dwelling." It paused to gaze intensely at me. "And I never said that He created me."

I speculated, though reaching, thinking that I might understand what it was getting at, "so you're saying we were created to contain you, in a sense?"

"No. Not at all," it snapped. The fire grew like a gathering wave, lighting the night enough to expose the outer trees of the forest off in the distance. "You are just a convenient harbor. Without me, you would never be." Its tone grew violent. "I have to exist. You are merely just a product of chance."

I noted the hint of anger that it tried to disguise but continued, "So, without us then, you can't live." I didn't know if I was stating a conclusion or asking a question.

"I can neither live or die. I am."

I felt that I was prematurely buried in its clever verbiage. Its words entombed me deep in a mud of confusion, yet paradoxically, I was on the verge of understanding.

I calmly and directly spoke, "I'm sorry. Please, go on."

It gleaned me over with enticing eyes, inviting me into its mind, "I will continue then."

"Besides contradicting that God is wholly good, the fact that I exist also reveals that He has limits, presenting a feasible concurrence that He is not omnipotent as well; at least not anymore, but I will speak of this later. Although, He is more powerful than you or anyone could ever possibly fathom. For example, your mind is capable of infinite possibilities and power. It was meticulously designed by Him. That alone should relate His superiority to everything. You are only utilizing a small portion of your entire brain's potential. This restriction to a mere fraction of its full power is His justly doing because the allowance of all its capabilities would only be a plague to your species; a fact realized through trial and error, for past experiments with ancient, mortal generations had failed."

"Within a short era of how your time is measured, because there was no domain of their brain that was kept from them, they completely decimated themselves from atrocities like war and genocide on scales magnified astronomically in comparison to anything your generations have ever seen or known of."

I listened. It is an arduous attempt to explain the complexity of what I had become. I was consumed and enchanted by everything that it was saying. It was as if an infectious seed of obsession had been planted and its words were caressing it into the soil of my loins, pushing me to yearn for what I lacked in knowledge.

I wanted to leave no crevice unchartered, so bluntly I asked it, "With that unlimited amount of power and freedom within us all, how could we fail at achieving universal harmony and prosperity? It is ignorance, along with limited and uncoerced thought that always damns us."

It chuckled audaciously and replied, "Maybe it could have been, or even could be, if not for me. I am, after all, the slimy skeletal hand pulling the rug from under order." It paused and held its hand out to me as if inviting me to dance. "I was about to explain this very detail. If you would like?"

"Yes," I said, fixated on its incandescent composure pouring out in the fire-light like some angelic creature.

It obligingly continued, "As I said, mortals only use a fraction of their mind. The rest of its wonder is cradled within what is like an induced coma, lulled into a deep slumber by its designer. Although, it must be acknowledged, that there are those of you that can produce sparks which ignite different areas of the brain. Because of its incomprehensible power, the sparks activating these shadow areas are reflexive outbursts from their dormitory slumber. It is the restricted subconscious reacting subconsciously. Experiencing these sparks allows these certain humans to enable actions perceived as supernatural, or by most of you, a hoax. If you see a woman communicating with the spirit world, you assume she is either a fraud or a witch, when she has only awoken a part of her mind that has been asleep but waiting, and it is within all of you. If you read of a young boy or girl that can bend spoons by willing it with his mind, I assure you that it is just real as I am."

It lit another cigarette and offered me another. I took it, mulling its words as it lit it for me.

"Do you still follow me, Argos?"

I nodded, dragging the smoke far into my lungs and exhaling it into the cold night. "I wish that you would call me by my name, though."

"I told you. This one fits you more properly." It puffed its cigarette deeply. The red glow of the cherry partially cast an ominous glow on its pale skin. The blood dried now into a stiff mask sticking to its face, reminding me of some barbaric warrior. "Shall we continue?"

"Of course."

"Splendid," it said as it allowed the smoke to escape its body. "We still have far to go before you completely understand. First, though, to help you along on your journey with me to the end, I must back-track a bit to the very beginning, to fill in a most important gap that we skipped."

Curiously, I nodded.

"You see," it stretched, "God is powerful, but not all-powerful, at least not anymore. Nor could He ever remain whole, for He was both good and evil. We are the definite powers of the universe which collide upon each other, incidentally, and we were once both of one. Being both made it difficult to create His world, for some of all of Him had to go into it. Otherwise, it would not be completely of Him. So, for the sake of His mortal creations, He separated Himself, dividing His good from me, sacrificing being all-powerful and whole.

You see, there is power in evil, just as there is power in good. He then hid me within the dormant sectors of the mind oblivious to stimuli. It is there, in the black spots of your conscious, that I hide like a serpent and wait. It is unfair when you think of it. Every other part of Him existing in harmony with His world, as I am stowed away. But all the same, I prefer it."

"You said that you wait. What do you wait for?" I asked respectively.

"I wait for those certain few to find me. And then I consume them."

I listened, imbibing every word. A prickling chill scoured my skin as it spoke that felt good. Its voice became deep, like distant thunder, and more alive than before. Its eyes had become even colder in the fire's incandescence. They burrowed like a worm into mine and forced me to hold my gaze. For the first time, since I saw it approach me like the crawling dead from a nightmare, I recognized fear stirring inside me again. The calmness I had felt was dissipating slowly. Though the unquenchable thirst for knowledge steered me still, I could sense resistance to its charismatic seduction stirring inside me. It was the will of my primordial fear.

"If you are found, then how?" I asked.

It frowned, briefly, but rebounded with a solemn tone that sometimes still haunts me no matter what I do to try and forget it. "You already know, Argos."

I stared back at it blankly.

It read my confusion correctly and continued to explain, "By passing through the shadow that veils me in the cellar of your minds."

"But how?" I demanded. "I got that much from what you said, but how?" I was beginning to feel the impatience drag me through a maze of broken glass.

It didn't seem to be bothered by my uneasiness and sharp demands. Instead calmly said, "Either by some horrible distress that fractures the mind and incidentally unlocks me. Even coping from some trauma, the mind can retreat to a place where it thinks that it is safe to hide from the world, unwittingly, delivering their conscious to me."

It smiled, pointing its finger at me. I noticed the blood that covered most of his hand up to his wrist. "Finally, my favorite. A way that you are familiar with. The way of freeing the constraints of the subconscious by altering the conscious, penetrating the shadow and finding me as I lie in solace, waiting." It grinned fiendishly and added, "Just as you once did."

I whispered, unhesitant and sure, "The dragon."

It manufactured a smarmy smirk as if intentionally revealing it still held a secret behind its eyes and said, "Yes." Once you were delivered into my place within yourself, you were foreshown everything. Gravely, I wanted to consume you; to allow you the taste of my power. But sadly, your mind is strong, and your natural defenses protected you. Sometimes the mortal mind is not ready to decay from within and become my playground. It is your conscious will. It is something that you, yourself, does not know is at work, protecting you when I am breathing close within. So, I relented my desire to wait for this night. If I could not have you, then I would take those close to you."

Anger rose in me; anger and guilt. This was my fault. If I had never broken through that night in the stranger's yard, then this would never have happened.

Unless, of course, it was lying. There was always that possibility. This could be a part of Jacob just having fun with me.

I had, after all, told the story of Lonnie Dade only a short time before.

I cleared my throat and not knowing why tried to conceal my doubt and said, "You're saying you knew this night would come."

"I know a lot of things," it said plainly, smiling as if we were enjoying a cup of tea in a café somewhere. "I knew that Jacob was the one who would need the key and that it was just a matter of time before he unlocked me." It looked around. "It all turned out quite nicely, I think."

I was becoming irked with its unctuous sincerity and kindness. I was beginning to feel as though I had been cajoled into some false state of security and comfort. Which, incidentally, scratched at the sore of my fear and made it bleed through me, for what is more frightening than wittingly falling under a spell of what you know to be already evil.

But I couldn't help it. Already I could feel its power easing me back into a comfortable kind of fear. Uncertainty and obliviousness to what was really happening somehow made me feel at ease. I continued to listen, ignoring my fear and latching onto its every word, feeling numb to anything real.

"For the last several years, I have watched you dabble in the pleasures of the world. You have always been drawing nigh to me while, little by little, you desperately molded a perception of yourself for others to see. All that time you were becoming old and useless in the most sacred part of you, your soul."

"You were the perfect pawn for me to manipulate. Once you gave him the drug and its potent effect began to stain his mind, I began luring him to the shadow; calling him from within the darkness. All the while I still had my tongue on you and your friend's minds, salivating upon your perceptions. I was thrilled when you told the detailed story of how I consumed Lonnie, starting with his mother and her mother before her. It brought back memories I had nearly lost – there have been so many like him and her. Fear and religion make for a great tool. His story, which you told so well, really blotted Jacob's mind and soaked into his conscious, spreading like a fatal disease. His perception of himself and reality took a noisome turn and allowed me to bask in the mayhem. It was the drug and your story that forced his mind to split and pull me from the shadow, incarnated as one of my most loyal puppets."

These ramblings that were tumbling into my ears made my mind hurt. Its impertinent countenance and tone made me feel as though I were a young boy getting dragged beneath my bed by some cold-handed fiend of hell.

Could anything this evil bastard was saying be true?

Was this truly the physical form of evil before me – smoking cigarettes and politely offering them to me? If so, then I assumed that it was safe to say that it was luring me into some spiritual snare to steal my soul by beguiling me with half-truths laced with this eternal wisdom.

Or it could be possible, also, that Jacob's mind had simply folded itself and crumpled like a used piece paper, then opened itself up again in a wrinkled and tattered state, no longer of any real use. It was quite possible that I was conversing with a tormented personality born already accustomed to hate and pain and violence because it was manifested in the shadow of an abandoned conscious, filtering the story of Lonnie Dade while splitting his mind.

It is more probable to be every one of these possibilities. I had somehow found myself in the eye of a perfect psychotic storm.

I could feel, though, that this was what it claimed to be no matter how well I tried to analyze it. It was pure, determined, evil staring me straight in the eyes. I had felt it long before it introduced itself, and heard it calling within me, screaming to tear itself through my head. I remember feeling its warm breath permeate within the cage of my conscious that it was locked in, desperate to escape. The memory of the way it fought and scratched to push through made me curious about what intentions it had for me.

Was it telling me these enchanting secrets only to soften my guard to take me over finally? Not slaughter me like it had my friends, but to inhale my entire being like the cigarette that it puffed casually.

It stared at me with wide, cantankerous eyes, which I felt more than I recognized. Its lips were curled in a wheedling pose, reminiscent of a royal prince's portrait hanging on a dingy castle wall. It appeared to be expecting from me some frivolous response, to devour it with its cunning tongue. I looked in its eyes, seeing Jacob's face, although, not a hint of his remnant stirred any longer. I dared not to deviate my gaze from its own entrapping stare and said plainly, "Are you going to eat me?"

A well-fabricated look of surprise stretched the skin across its face, and it leaned forward, within only inches of me. "Eat you?" It spoke with a teasing rasp; its gore-splattered face held a strong countenance. "Well, that really depends." It leaned back and folded its hands comfortably in its lap, smirking fiendishly.

"Depends on what?" I asked.

It responded, "Most of all, you."

The fire was still a fervid storm, burning like a livid deity. The night remained cool and crisp, biting at my skin. Behind the evil, the endless crackle of the coals incinerating in the fire-pit echoed through the open field and throughout the thick woods. Somewhere in the belly of those woods, cloaked in its darkness, an owl hooted at the high, peering moon.

Beneath the growl of the flames, almost inaudible, but recognizable, I heard a feeble moan. My eyes shifted excitedly to Lena and saw her body weakly rising as she breathed shallow gasps. She was lying on her back still, bloody and badly beaten. Her face was swollen as if grossly affected by dozens of tumors disfiguring her features. She was slowly regaining consciousness as her arms and feet shuffled aimlessly, tenderly moaning. She was not yet fully awake, but in the purgatory realm in between.

I noticed that the evil hadn't bothered to look at her, perhaps it had already expected this. Instead, it held its clutching stare on me, somehow applying pressure on my chest. "Would you like to save her?" It asked.

The question took me by surprise, but I answered without hesitation. "Of course I would."

It skipped its eyes to where Hess' body lay in a fetal-like pose; his head empty of brains and matter from the large hole put there by the evil. Without uttering another word it stood up smoothly, breathing through its mouth softly, yet audible, and walked over to where the body lay. It picked up the stone lying in a soup of gore and chunks of a skull, then carried it over to where Lena moaned, dragging its dead foot across the dirt.

"What are you doing?" I barked in anger. I tried to stand again, but the pain in my knee snatched me back down. Not even the flow of adrenaline surging through me could stop the pain. I wailed sharply.

"Stay right there, Argos. You could never stop me if you wanted to, even with a good knee."

There was a distinct, crippling kind of panic and worry that turned my innards into stone. It is a feeling that possesses horrible qualities difficult to describe. More adrenaline sucker-punched my heart as I watched it raise the soccer ball sized stone over her head. All I could do was scream in raging overtones of fear. "What are you doing? Stop it! Kill me you coward! I'm right here!"

It laughed maliciously, holding the stone over her face ready to thrust it through her skull at any moment. "Argos, do you think that I could not do that at any moment of my choosing if I wanted to? I could, right this very instance, crush her pretty little face and come eat your pounding heart right from your chest without wasting a single breath from this body."

It paused and watched her squirm beneath him, oblivious to the danger hovering above her. Then it continued to speak, still infatuated by her it seemed, "But as I said, it is up to you whether you live or die tonight. I will also allow the chance to save her as well." It drew away its playful gaze from Lena and found me, grinning a clever grin and added, "All that you have to do is answer a riddle,"

Its condescending tone and straight-forward attitude annoyed me greatly. A molten stream of anger ran through and ravaged me within. I wanted to leap to my feet and prod my thumbs deep into its eyeballs, scooping them away in a fit of curses with spit flying and falling from my mouth.

I had never felt so helpless, afraid, and disgustingly angry to the extreme I experienced sitting in the cold at that moment, meddling in the presence of evil; all of them consuming me at the same time.

Vehemently I roared at it, "This isn't a fucking game!"

Calmly, unscathed emotionally, by my passionate outburst it said, "Oh, but it is. This is my favorite game, actually. I play it often, every few thousand years, or so. I do, however, arrange the rules here and there to better suit specific personalities, but basically, they are the same. It remains a game, my game in fact. Do you not want to play? Or do you …," It gestured the stone, showing it to me as if I had forgotten that it could break her face at any moment.

I felt instinctively that it was best to be as cool as my riled emotions would allow, so to not cause any situation that could lead to the stone being dropped, of course.

"Yes," I said. "Anything. Just please put down the rock."

"I will. When you answer the riddle."

"Jesus Christ!" I shouted, losing my cool just that quickly. "Then fucking tell me already!"

"Okay, okay," it said laughing antagonistically at the bold eagerness leaping out of me to save my friend. "Just remember that you must answer correctly, or else." Its eyes swayed to the stone, then to Lena.

Already feeling benighted and beaten emotionally, I searched myself inside for confidence hopefully hiding in me. If it was it there, it was buried deep,

"I know," I said staring at Lena trying to wake to this terror. Stay asleep, please." I thought, "Stay asleep Lena."

CHAPTER 19

A Conundrum

It cradled the stone with both hands just over its head. If dropped, the point of impact was the center of Lena's face. It looked at me and then to her as she scuffled about below, then back to me again. It smiled warmly and said, "Okay then. Here it is."

"You have been locked in a concrete box, never mind how you got there, just know that you are there. Surrounding you on all sides are thick walls. There are no windows or doors; no trap doors of any kind, either. Only concrete. Inside, there is a mirror and a wooden table. Never mind how it got there, they just are. So tell me, Argos, how do you get out of the room?"

At first, I thought the evil was severely fucking with me. Of course, I supposed that it had been fucking with me from the beginning with its deviant trickery, attempting to persuade me to feel compassion and contentment in its presence. But for a moment, I felt that surely this entire charade had been a joke; there couldn't be a real answer to the riddle, could there? Why a riddle in the first place?

What did any of this mean? Could it be that this evil, if indeed that is what it really was, was insane? Could evil have gone insane? If so, then what did that mean?

Its next words, though, confirmed the seriousness of it all. "You should hurry, Argos. This is becoming heavy, and I doubt she is quick enough to move out of the way if it happens to slip."

It was no joke.

I could see by the glow of the fire, tracing her outline on the ground, that she was awakening. Her eyes were not open; in fact, they were swollen shut and gashed quite badly. Her soft moans had become more pronounced, and her movement seemed to be more controlled than the clumsy flailing she had started with. The stone was like an impending doom cradled over her by the bough of its grasp.

The riddle scraped its talons in my mind. I tried to find an acceptable answer, but all I could think of was the macabre image of the stone pummeling through Lena's face and smashing her mouth. I imagined her teeth breaking free from their roots in her gums and with all the spit, combined with blood, becoming lodged in the back of her throat, like a clogged drain, choking her within seconds.

All of this was unless, of course; the stone would just burst her head open like an eggshell.

Frustrated and scared, unsure of anything still, I said "Through the mirror. I would go through the mirror."

It seemed disappointed and shook its head emphatically. "No Argos. You are a more clever creature than that. Remember that I dwell within you too and know everything about you. I happen to know that riddles are what you love, as do I. That is why I am giving you this opportunity." It exasperated a long, drawn sigh and continued, "I know that you are under a lot of pressure, so for that reason I will allow you to try again. But, I am warning you, hurry. Lena is beneath even more than you. It is getting too much for me to bear as well." It pretended to drop the instrument of death, but caught it just before it left its hands and shattered her face.

I was furious at evil for what it was doing and for what it had done. I was enraged at myself, as well, for not being able to see the answer. I hated the pain I was in. I didn't know where to begin to decipher such a maniacal predicament. Aggravated and full of contempt for everything, I stammered, "There is no fucking answer! It is impossible."

"You must not think literally," it explained. "The answer is beyond what you observe and interpret as possible. It is abstract; you must think outside the chosen realm of normality."

It stared at me. A viscous, untamed, trace of eternal wisdom glimmered in its stare. The wisdom of all that was ever good and ever evil. In that stare, I felt I knew that it wanted me to know the answer. It was as if the answer was the 'why' to everything and it wanted me to understand.

And then it came like a warm, comforting rain on a winter day. I was taken by complete surprise. It was as if the answer had appeared in my thoughts like an apparition out of a dark closet. I mulled it carefully and quickly, though it seemed that it was wrong I knew it was right.

"Okay, okay. I know," I said assuredly.

"I am certain that you hope so. I am also certain that Lena does as well." It looked down upon her body shifting in tiny gestures trying to regain her motor senses. Her eyes were still closed; still shielded from the evil preying over her. It then said sternly, "Very well. What is your answer?"

"You have to look in the mirror and see what you saw. You then grab the 'saw' and cut the table in half. Two halves then make a whole, so you put them together and crawl through the 'hole.' " I then took a deep, regenerative breath as the world seemed to flip back to sane again. I knew I had solved it.

It tossed the bloody stone safely away from Lena's face. Her eyes were now open, and she deliriously sobbed from either the pain raking deep in her body, or the trauma from awaking from a nightmarish memory. She grabbed at the soil with loose, lost fists trying to find something to hold onto.

It clapped its hands together with a redundant, slow beat "That is very clever, Argos. I am impressed. Although, I knew that you could do it." It peered at me with a hardened gaze. Its eyes were now famished of life and the moon cast a dirty, ghostly, glow upon the black circles around them. A sinister, vampiric grin erased the cold sternness of its face as it stated bluntly, "Now. Answer the riddle."

The relief I had felt began to ebb faintly like the flavor of some sweet candy. Apprehension and an obtuse kind of paranoia began to permeate like a seeping gas within me.

What did it mean by this? I had solved the dirty motherfucker's riddle.

I had an ominous feeling constricting my nerves and the reliable intuition that I would find out very soon what it all meant.

"What?" I said with a strange overtone of defeat.

Suddenly, its stare told me I was nothing more than some diseased mutant and of no use to it any longer. I wanted to lash out at it, even if it meant killing Jacob.

Angrily and defensive I blurted, "I solved your goddamn riddle. What else is there?"

"You did solve it. Yes," it agreed. "But you did not answer yet. That was the bargain, and you are half-way there. By answering it, you must tell me what it means. What is the answer?"

"But that's crazy! It's just a riddle! It means absolutely nothing!"

"Everything means something," it hissed in a raised, malevolent tone.

The moon was like an angel's fiery-white face wrapped tightly by the deep, smoke colored clouds that shone over its right shoulder in the black sky.

"Even if it is nothing to you, it is always something to someone else; and incidentally, is something to you because it is something from you."

"Jacob," Lena's voice trembled in the cold night as she continued to writhe on the ground like a dead snake. Her tone was weak and powerless. The pain she was absorbing through her wounds was evident in her speech. She sobbed deeply from it. In the fire-light, I could see the various sized chunks, that were pooled with blood, torn from her skin gaping in her body. Her pain made me want to cry.

"Jacob," she sounded groggy and confused. "What happened?" She breathed lightly between tiny cries. The twisting rips of agony were undoubtedly pervading her senses now in the eve of consciousness.

It ignored her and stared at me voraciously. The appeasing countenance that it previously portrayed had vanished, and now menacingly it said, "Your time is almost up."

It was at this moment that the trees guarding the north end of the clearing, at the vicinity of the lone entrance, began to shimmer and blink radiantly. Strobes of blue flashed like flares of lightning in the darkness, displaying a beautiful portrait of light and shadows fighting against each other.

The evil cocked its gaze and saw the lights painting the trees. "Ahh, the balance." It was as calm as the water behind me, speaking with a tranquil flow of words that were expressed precisely and perfectly. "It would seem your dear friend Lena managed to dial the police before I got hold of her. I shall explain, then, seeing that time is fading."

There was no illusion that I had any real choice. I nodded my head, agreeing silently, for I was deeply unnerved and afraid of what revelation it may bestow.

Still looming over Lena, who was reeling sadly in confusion and pain like a scavenger sniffing its spoil in the wild, it sighed and began. "The man trapped in the box is real. The box is real. The table and the mirror are real. But the answer, Argos, is very much an illusion."

Two police cars, with their lights flashing silently, became visible at the top of the hill. Their headlights cut through the terror that had couched the night like an angel's presence in Hell. I could hear the idling engines purr as they parked in the distance.

The evil remained focused only on me.

It continued, "Unlike himself and the box, the hole that he creates is not real. The man uses his mind to escape, and the safety to which he finds is only a manifested perception of reality. He is still trapped and always will remain apart from his manifestation. He can only dream of freedom because he never left. And most assuredly the inevitability of death is real."

It paused, looking down at Lena with a disturbed, hungry smile stretching its face into a contorted pose.

"Jacob. I'm hurt. Please help me," she said beginning to gain what little strength she could inhale. Her voice sounded clearer, although it was still pitted with pain. She reached blindly for its leg, trying to find security and comfort.

I heard two car doors slam shut from on the hill. The light bars on their roofs sprayed flashes of blue everywhere, provoking hope. Two flashlights came to life and bounce around spastically down the hill.

"Lena, it's okay. Don't move," I coaxed. She tried to move her head in the direction of my voice, but a gash in her neck prevented her.

"Who is that? Hess? Oh God, Hess. I'm Hurt. Please help me." Her words came in syllables struggling to fall in line.

It continued to speak as if there had never been an interruption. Its inane eyes were already burying me in their darkness. "Do you understand the answer? Do you see that you are the man?"

Half-way down the hill now, I heard Sheriff Khan shout, "Jacob is that you?" Their flashlights danced in the black void beyond the fire, getting closer. But not close enough.

"Do you see now that there is no hope? No escaping," it said balefully.

As it spoke it lifted Jacob's boot over Lena's face. I heard her last anguished gasp for air just before the heel of the boot stomped the center of her face. The front of her skull and nose cracked beneath the force, sounding like snow crunching under the sole of a boot. Her body methodically went limp and lifeless, then creeks of blood seeped down the side of her face, matting her hair in the dirt.

"Did you just see that?" The deputy, Chase, shouted in disbelief from afar. "What the fuck did he do? "

"Jacob," his father called out, now getting close enough to see that there was something afoul. Something sinister and unfathomable. He reached to his holster, instinctively, and let his hand feel the butt of his gun.

"Fucking hell, Sheriff! Jesus, that's a girl! He crushed her goddamn face with his boot." Chase spoke with an extremely drawn southern accent, like a trailer park version of Andy Griffith. He lifted his gun quickly and aimed it at the evil as they crept closer, now only thirty or forty feet away.

"Don't you dare fire that weapon at my son!" Sheriff Kahn shouted.

Still, it never broke its gaze from me. Even as it removed the boot from the hole in Lena's face, it held firm its stare. Like the dragon from my vision, it wanted me desperately and would stop at nothing to devour me inside and out.

It began to move towards me with that same zombie-like limp. Its foot was twisted sideways and stiffened rigorously; it slid across the dirt, snooping towards me. I could hear it breathing. The noise of rolling thunder growling in its belly gave my mind a sensitive tingle. Smoke seemed to spill like gusts of steam from its nostrils. Its eyes became slits and yellow with decaying mortality. A forked tongue, drenched and dripping with blood, stretched towards me, twitching like a dying worm.

It had found me, and now it had me.

I couldn't tell what was real and was meant to be real. My mind was rolling over itself, still, from the drug and all I wanted was for everything to stop.

But it wouldn't. This was what was real.

Regardless of whether it was really morphing into a sadistic, predatory serpent or not, it was still coming at me. That much I was sure, and that it wanted to eat me.

Sheriff Kahn and Deputy Chase appeared out of the cloak of night and stepped deeper into the glowing pool of light. With his hand still on his gun nestled in its holster Sheriff Kahn spoke with a shaky voice. "What's going on Jacob? Are you okay, son? We got a call from Lena's mother who said she was coming out here. I knew you would be here. Why did you lie, son?"

"Your son is in the comfort of death, Sheriff," the evil said, rasping every syllable.

All the color melted away and left his face as disgust rummaged him throughout when he finally noticed all the death. His mouth dropped open as his eyes reluctantly scanned the scene. All the blood spilled into the dirt had become a thick sludge of gore by the heat of the flames.

With his gun still drawn and pointed at the evil limping towards me, I heard Chase vomit violently and cry, "Jesus on a fucking stick, Sheriff! What do I do?"

Sheriff Kahn looked distraught, unsure of what to do next. He bit his lip and wiped sweat from his brow, then choked by emotion he said, "Jacob! Jacob, son! What did you do? Turn around and look at me!"

The evil ignored him and slinked nearer to me. The urge to rip away the flesh in my throat and eat it shone through in its intense gaze.

"He killed them all! He fucking ate them, man!" I yelled as I tried to back away clumsily, using my hands and arms to slide my ass backward across the ground. "Just shoot him! Do you hear me? Shoot him!"

Evil was right on top of me, reaching out for me like the silent creature, Nosferatu.

"Sheriff?" Chase squeaked while nervously aiming his gun.

The first shot rang out. I jumped from the initial shock. A part of me seemed to leave my body in some stellar act of cowardice portrayal by my inner self. The bullet tore through the back of its right shoulder and blew a hole the size of a half-dollar out of the front. Blood and pieces of wet flesh spit like a rabid animal from the gaping mess. I heard the bullet splash in the pond behind me.

The deputy lowered his gun and put his free hand to his face. "Holy shit! You shot him, Sheriff."

"It's not my son," the Sheriff said still pointing his gun, smoke swirled out from the barrel.

It turned around unfazed by the bullet and huffed its imperial breath coarsely. It began to limp again, stalking towards the sheriff.

"Oh shit! Sir, do you want me to shoot him? The deputy's hands trembled. His eyes were wide and had been thoroughly raped by terror. "Look at that sir. He's got goddamn blood all over his face. What the hell is happening?"

The sheriff ignored Chase's comical rambling and said to the evil, "Jacob! Stop! Stop right there!"

It inched closer to them, breathing laboriously. Behind guttural gasps, it hissed, "You are going to have to kill me, daddy."

"Son. Please . . . , stop!" The sheriff forced himself to glance at the bodies, mutilated, half-eaten and left to spoil in the night. "Whatever you've done, Jacob, we can fix this. Please, though, you have to stop."

It scooped up the robust stick Hess had used to break my knee and raised it forth, threatening to strike. Blood was beginning to soak Jacob's Pearl Jam shirt from the heavy flow out of the hole in his chest.

"Kill your boy, daddy. Look at what he has done," it taunted. It shuffled hurriedly towards the sheriff and spat out a Celtic scream with a deep penetrating tone that seemed to have been born by the loins of Cerberus, the hound of Hades, and it lunged its arms forward to swing the stick, channeling every ounce of its strength.

The second shot clattered the silence around us. It exploded, gratuitously, through the back of its left leg, chopping the feral demon to the ground. Blood flew in a fantastic spray of black mist in the feverish glow like some graphic scene in a cartoon. I immediately tasted metal as my face was showered by the warm splatter.

Chase rushed over to where it laid bleeding and fell to his knees, scrambling for his handcuffs. He wrestled them onto its hands chanting, "Jesus Christ and Holy shit!"

Sheriff Kahn fell where he stood and cried. His gun that fired the bullet which tore through his son's flesh fell to the ground. He wept with intense fervor, the way no father should ever have to.

It laid in the dirt, adjoined by Helen's stiff carcass not far beside it. It was handcuffed and bleeding profusely. The glow emitting from the fire captured its horrible grin as it laughed maniacally like some brain-damaged clown.

Over and over it sang a whispering tune, "Only an illusion. Only an illusion."

CHAPTER 20

Decryption

In the years since that dire night at the water's edge of the pond, I've examined every explanation attainable through logic to refute what it is that I genuinely believe, that what I saw and conversed with was, in fact, evil. I've entertained the possibility that Jacob had had a severely torturous trip that carved a particularly jagged persona from his fragile psyche.

For weeks following the murders, I even foolishly hoped to awaken somewhere discovering that it all had been my imagination fabricating the diabolically fantastical occurrence. There was a short time that I even gained small portions of peace inside myself by falsely affirming that the evil which manifested itself, using Jacob as a communicable conduit to reach me, was only him and not a malicious part of God.

If only I were naïve enough to believe it had been a psychotic snap brought on by the acid like everyone else, I could rest without terror opening its bleeding eyes in my dreams.

The problem I face with knowing the truth is that I can never forget the presence. It was the calm and quiet darkness it emitted that soaked my spirit that hasn't yet dried which confirms in me that it was no hallucinogenic hoax. Face to face and succumbed by its power, it was almost as if I were in Eden holding the forbidden fruit in my hand while salivating with an animalistic quality.

There is no question as to whether I spoke with evil or not. It shared with me divine secrets that should be forgotten, but will never be. The knowledge that we have all been anathematized by our Creator will only generate fear and paranoia but is the truth all the same.

If only I had augured the phantasm that haunted me in the stranger's yard, then maybe, none of the horrors would've taken place. Further scrutiny of the hallucinogenic dream from that night has led me to believe that it was a prophetic message riddled with imaginative symbolism ripe for deciphering. Undoubtedly, it was bestowed by the evil that was lingering in a subconscious prison as some sort of jeer at my faltering sanity. It was during that cryptic premonition that the webby gossamer separating myself from the shadow's realm in my mind (in all our minds) was peeled away and torn like a bleeding scab.

In that state of conscious bloodshed all had been revealed, but I didn't see it. I wrote it off as some crazed, morbid, and beautiful nightmare that was no more than a fun tale to recite around bonfires. It wasn't until after that terrible night that I recognized it was a divine vision, an egregious prophecy that shall haunt me till no end. Its vivid voraciousness has gnawed a scar within my psyche that I recognize yet can't control. The dragon lives in me still. I feel its breath warming my every thought.

The screaming face, burning from Heaven as it fell, was God injecting Himself into the world so that His presence could be present within it always. He crashed as if within a fiery chariot, the awesome bang of His entire being exploding into an illusory eruption of spewing colors permeated throughout existence and was then imbibed by it. I'll never forget the strange warmth that confused me as the colors bled like rain from the clouds and covered me along with everything.

The face was only the start of this allegorical journey. I'm sure that everything I was shown had some meaning, but my mind can only unravel pieces of it. I could be reaching, but I am convinced otherwise, based on my experiences. Respectfully, it was I that experienced them and only I that can determine anything.

The frog slithering like a weary snail in the black pool of grass was the external visage of my conscious, the conduit to the shadow. It is fascinating to think that somehow, being that it was my incognizant subconscious generating the symbolic revelation under the authority of some ancient deviant, I was capable of following my conscience without ever knowing it was my own.

The tranquil room, ranting wildly with calm white lights and marked by unfamiliar symbols of some far-off language, was the gossamer fabric sheathing the shadow as I passed through. It seems that it was a clever disguise of the actual lair made by the evil as to retain my limited mind's compacity and conserve strength within my subconscious for the complete mind-fuck it was about to endure. Knowing that if after initially entering that unchartered realm of the mind I was immediately struck with lucid visions of mayhem and horror I would undoubtedly become useless and catatonic, it prepared a place of false serenity for me to become quickly comfortable within. This way I could slowly adapt to the demise of sanity as I was delivered unto a slow-paced psychosis without being aware; much like the parable of the frog in a pot of water as it is gradually heated to boil.

Reflecting, it was the woman that grips my soul more than anything, even more so than the dragon. I believe her to have been the representation of God as both good and evil; beautiful and ugly. This would explain the over-powering enchantment she cast over my spirit. Perhaps, even, she was the exquisite delineation of the anima archetype in the back of my psyche's throat. I remember the feeling of splendor within me as she magically floated like an angel in a dream. I also recall the punishing terror that scathed my soul as she transformed into the ghoulish fiend. Her transformation, allegorically, was the prophetic declaration of what would become of Jacob.

Her blood symbolized the ablutionary agent for transcendence. It was the potent mind-juice which stimulated my conscious to a more heightened susceptibility. It was in this whimsical fantasy that the acid had directed me to the shadow. Without it, the shadow would have only been a cloud within the dark matter of my brain. And the evil may have never set its sights on me to destroy my life one friend at a time.

The portal of chaos, fathomed by the blood, in the wall swirling into some awkward abyss with voices clamoring in agony on the other side of the tenuous skin-like barrier was the cursed pit of my subconscious. It is from here where demons escape. It is the place that spoils the soul, all the things hidden by the shadow.

Antiquated and ubiquitous the evil was the great dragon. Because this haunting prophetic dream has compelled my thoughts in a way akin to the obsession I have been able to glean many allegorical aspects from this particular piece of it all. The fact is that I was somehow cognizant within the parameter of my subconscious experiencing and witnessing, unwittingly, the manifested secrets give me the unique affliction of remembering how the intention of the revelation felt to help me ascertain the meaning through reverie.

Although as terrifying as it was, hissing vulgarly and yearning for me, the dragon was bound by strings initially during my encounter. It is logical to gather that this illustrates, as the evil in Jacob had told me, how God hid and buried it in a dark tomb within our mind, keeping it at bay although not eradicated, for it must still exist for God to exist in our world; for He is all. I remember the raw fear that paralyzed me as its eyes devoured me, wanting me. It wasn't until the crone spat her blood upon its broken carcass, resurrecting it and freeing it from the constraints, unleashing a vile terror, much like our act of dropping the acid. The memory of these fears reveals to me much more than any visual memory available in the recesses of my mind.

Finally, the portrait that revealed me, painted by the blood cascading down the wall, was my mind's eye entombed by the powerful liquid having its way with me like a horny primate.

It was my subliminal awareness revealing itself to me.

EPILOGUE

Evil. It is a vile presence that resides in us all. It pervades, inconspicuously, everything we know and want to know, even everything we never knew we don't know.

It is what orchestrated everything. It was it that gave me the horrid vision, letting me know without me knowing, and it was it that ascended upon us all that ghastly night. It was the tireless work of it that coerced Jacob's mind into breaking free from the chains of reality. It showed his susceptible psyche how to grab hold of the imaginary perception illustrated by his mind of Lonnie Dade when hearing the tale and allowed him to physically and literally become the damaged persona.

At the same time, it revealed itself and its secrets to me. Even though Chris was already on the proverbial verge of madness without the assistance of LSD, he was by no means a savage psycho. It was the same evil that permeated Hess and Jacob, impregnating them with its presence while making itself known in my mind, that overtook him. It is hidden, and it is real. That truth is what will eternally haunt me. The shadow is there; it always has been. We don't have to evolve to reach it and step through; instead, we evolve the moment we reach it.

To this day, Jacob Kahn calls the Keffling State Asylum for the Criminally Insane his home. He can never be alone with anyone. It is said that he speaks in wonderful and awful riddles that ignite the curious senses of the mind, but sadistically he maneuvers his words to create sedition within the structural fabric of logic.

He still walks crookedly, carrying the dead weight of his right leg.

The End

ABOUT THE AUTHOR

H.D. Kirkland, III resides in Headland, Alabama with his wife Amy and their four children. He studied at Troy University and has true love for animals and baseball.

Made in the USA
Columbia, SC
16 November 2022

71081694R00112